To Darcy,
Thanks so much for the support.

Terry L. McBride

THE SEASONS OF SOLOMON

Terry McBride

ISBN 978-1-68526-444-4 (Paperback)
ISBN 978-1-68526-446-8 (Hardcover)
ISBN 978-1-68526-445-1 (Digital)

Copyright © 2022 Terry McBride
All rights reserved
First Edition

All rights reserved. No part of this publication may be reproduced, distributed, or transmitted in any form or by any means, including photocopying, recording, or other electronic or mechanical methods without the prior written permission of the publisher. For permission requests, solicit the publisher via the address below.

Covenant Books
11661 Hwy 707
Murrells Inlet, SC 29576
www.covenantbooks.com

CHAPTER 1

It is winter 1972 in west Detroit, Michigan. There has been heavy snowfall in these two weeks prior to the Christmas celebration. All houses, trees, and streets are covered with snow. On the end of the block sits an old, boarded-up, abandoned house. If you follow the sounds of laughter into the structure, there you would find eight-year-old Solomon Phelps and Otis Easton, playing a game of "cops and robbers," catch me if you can.

The two boys are dressed in heavy winter garments. They run in opposite directions through the old house. Scurrying through the many passages of this structure, they find themselves face-to-face. Solomon draws a toy gun from his inner jacket and aims it at Otis.

"Bang, you're dead. I told you not to mess with this bad cop."

Otis grabs his chest, falling to the floor and making groaning sounds.

"What did you do that for?"

Both burst into laughter, Solomon helps Otis to his feet, and the game ensues again. They take off running until loose floorboards slip underfoot, revealing the corpse of a young woman. The corpse of the young woman under the floorboards is wrapped in plastic. The woman's face and upper body are exposed. She is pretty, twenty, and dressed in a type of work uniform. There is a name tag attached to her blouse. It reads, "AIMEE."

The boys are both afraid and excited at the same time. They loved the idea of solving a murder mystery; however, they knew that this was real, and the killer could be close by. With a bit of trembling, the boys look at each other.

Otis asks, "Who is she? Is she dead?"

Solomon replies, "Yes, of course, she's dead. She's frozen solid."

Simultaneously they exclaim.

"We better go tell somebody."

Otis and Solomon take off running until they reached the crack in the door from which they had initially entered. They slosh through the snow while admiring all the neighborhood's elaborate Christmas lights and various decorations. There is only one house that sits between the abandoned structure and Solomon's residence. Solomon lives there with his maternal grandmother, Ernestine Phelps (aka Granny), and his mother, Agnes Phelps. That very same night, Ernestine Phelps (Granny) is getting ready to head to church for a weekly Bible study. This fifty-year-old grandmother bundles herself in outer garments. She looks around her immaculately kept home while putting final touches on it.

She straightens pictures on the wall and dusts the mantel in the living room. She then grabs her purse, books, and Bible from the coffee table, near the sofa. Then Granny walks to the front window and peers out. She can see little

Solomon and Otis rushing toward home. Granny begins to whisper a prayer to the Lord as the boys rush in. Solomon and Otis track the front entrance with snow and slush. Granny has a scowl across her face.

Solomon asks, "Granny, who are you talking to?"

"I was talking to the Lord, baby."

Looking around, Solomon replies, "I don't see anyone. Where is the Lord?"

"He is everywhere, baby. Now can you explain to me why the two of you are coming in so late?"

Otis frantically tries to explain. "We were trying to solve the case of the dead lady."

"Oh, my Lord! Are you saying that you saw a dead woman?"

Otis responds, "Yes, ma'am, in that raggedy old house down the street."

Solomon adds, "Yes, Granny, we joke often but not this time. Otis almost knocked me down trying to run from her."

Otis shoves Solomon, "I'm not afraid of dead people."

"Listen to me. You, boys, stay away from that old house. Do you understand me? There is always something going on over there."

Solomon inquires, "But, Granny, what about the dead lady?"

"You let me worry about that. Otis, is your mother at home?"

"Yes, ma'am."

"Good. Come on you two."

They follow Granny out of the front door and onto the porch. Granny instructs Solomon.

"Solomon, go home with Otis. Ruby can look after you until your mother gets home."

Granny watches the boys cross the street until they enter Ruby's home. Ruby waves at Granny, then closes the door, entering the home. Granny moves in closer to the porch banister while looking down the street with expectation. She speaks aloud to herself. "I wish your mother would stay home sometimes."

In the distance, Granny can see her daughter, Agnes (thirty), approaching. With some difficulty, she lightly jogs through the snow down the sidewalk. She is wearing a rabbit fur jacket but is otherwise skimpily dressed in a short skirt and boots. As she moves in closer, Granny says aloud, "Here she comes now."

Arriving at the house Agnes says, "Hey, Mom, sorry if I made you late for Bible study again." Agnes climbs the stairs and embraces Granny.

"You and Deacon Hodges. He's late again too."

Just then a van turns unto their street. Deacon Hodges pulls the Van over and parks in front of the Phelps' home. The van is full of elderly passengers. Deacon Hodges rolls down the window. "Ready to go, Mother Phelps?"

"Yes, I've been ready."

She climbs into the van. Agnes watches as the van pulls off. She hollers.

"Say a prayer for me, Mom."

Granny whispers to herself, "I always do, child. I always do."

Arriving at the House of Praise Christian Ministries church, Deacon Hodges pulls up in front to give all passengers quick access to the sanctuary. He then parks and follows behind them. The elderly bunch rush into the sanctuary where Pastor Oscar Sullivan, fifty and casually dressed, stands before a small gathering of members. An organist plays "Amazing Grace" softly.

Pastor speaks, "While we await the arrival of our other members, are there any prayer requests?"

Sister Mitchell raises her hand. "I have finals coming up."

Deacon Hodges, Granny, and the others entering are all finding seats. As Granny takes her seat in the pew just in front of sister Mitchell, she replies, "Pray that the violence in our neighborhood will cease. And you all know my daughter, Agnes. I don't even have to say it. Just continue to pray for her."

Sister Mitchell places her hand on Granny's shoulder. "You know we will, Granny."

"Yes, and of course, you know about my grandson."

There is light giggling heard from the members.

Granny continues, "That boy—"

The members simultaneously finish her sentence. "Is going to be a preacher someday."

Granny interjects, "Yes, he is. He knows his Bible better than most grown folks, and he's only eight."

Sister Mitchell wraps her arms around Granny. "You are so right, Granny. God has a plan for his life."

Granny nods her head in agreement.

"Now, Pastor, where did we stop last week?"

Pastor Sullivan moves behind his podium and opens his Bible. "We will continue our studies in the book of Ecclesiastes, chapter three. First, will everyone please stand for a word of prayer?"

All the members stand, hold hands, and bow their heads. Pastor Sullivan prays, "Lord, please hear our prayers. Be with Sister Mitchell as she prepares for finals, and we pray that you will guide little Solomon to the place in life where he can best serve you."

They all shouted, "Amen!"

CHAPTER 2

Twenty-five years later, two illustrious gentlemen in business attire, Detectives Solomon Phelps and Otis Easton cruise the old neighborhood. The vehicle is an elaborate black luxury car. The police radio blares officer activity in the area. Otis is the driver and Solomon stares out of the passenger side window. Red and blue lights lay in the rear window. A detective's badge lay open on the front seat. A Bible engraving reads, "Solomon Phelps." A lit cigar lay in an ashtray. Otis lifts the cigar. Annoyed by the smoke, Solomon sighs and rolls down his window.

"Remember when we used to play cops and robbers on these very streets?"

Otis takes a puff and then responds, "Like it was yesterday."

The neighborhood is run down. A rusty old gate still stands and encloses a rubbish-filled yard where the old boarded-up house once stood.

Reminiscing, Solomon replies, "So they finally tore that old house down."

Otis pulls closer to see tiny grave markers. He then says to Solomon, "Do you see those little markers? The neighborhood kids bury their pets there."

Solomon asks, "Like in the movie?"

Laughing, Otis responds, "No, at least I hope nothing is coming back from the dead."

Solomon's facial expression changes to somber as he asks a question. "Do you remember the time when we found that dead woman?"

Otis nods yes. They look at each other and ponder the memory of that day. Otis and Solomon's thoughts take them back twenty-five years to the boarded-up, old, abandoned house without the tiny tombstones. Clear in their minds is the image of the female corpse under the floorboards. As their thoughts return to the present, Solomon states.

"It's strange that it hadn't crossed my mind until now, but I wonder if that case was ever solved."

"I don't know. That was a long time ago."

There is complete silence as they continue their cruise of the old neighborhood in deep thought. What they had not yet seen were the names on the tiny markers. A closer look would have revealed the names on several little tombstones. "Pepper sleeps here," "RIP Goldie," "Abbott Gerbil III," "Mr. Bird," and "Aimee."

*****

Early the next morning, Solomon and Otis climb the stairs to the Police Station entrance. At the top of the stairs, yet off to the side, is Bernard Burgess. He is a heavyset man, thirty, and dressed in business attire. He studies Otis and Solomon, but they do not notice him. A dozen cadets in sweatpants and T-shirts jog down the stairs and up the street.

Otis chuckles. "So do you think any of those guys will survive the academy?"

Solomon explains, "The numbers have been narrowing down every week. We shall soon see." Otis attempts to be funny. "Some of them look too old. And others are just a little too thick around the mid-section."

The two detectives enter the building. Continuing their conversation on the way to their desks, Solomon says, "Nowadays, people will take a job they don't like just to pay the bills. Although I get that, how much integrity really goes into it?"

Before Otis answers, his attention is drawn to an attractive secretary that crosses their path on her way to an office. Now staring at the woman, Otis replies, "None at all, but I am a man of integrity. Don't you agree?"

Solomon smirks and retorts. "Let me save you some time, Otis. That looks like a smart lady right there, and I'm sure that she can spot a player."

Officers, Detectives, and others in the main lobby burst into laughter and make wise cracks. In response, Otis says loudly to Solomon, "Oh, I'm a player? Well, at least I'm still in the game. Everyone knows that Crystal has you on a leash." Solomon appears embarrassed.

*****

In a diner across town, Crystal and Pam, two attractive and well-dressed women in their thirties, are seated near a window, having breakfast. Crystal watches as people pass by the window. Pam draws her attention by asking a question, "So has Solomon proposed yet?"

Crystal responds, "Proposed?"

"Yes, proposed. It's about time, don't you think?"

Crystal ignores Pam and turns her attention back to the people on the streets.

Pam chuckles, snaps her fingers, and exclaims, "Hello. Earth to Crystal."

"What!?

"You don't listen. I told you what you need to do."

"I was listening to you then and now, Pam. But do you know how long it's been since I have been to church?"

"Well, that is where you met him."

"Pam, I have to get myself together first. I certainly hope that you don't think that Solomon is a saint either. He has some issues of his own, you know."

"Crystal, you are my best friend, and I'm just trying to look out for you. Because you know—"

Crystal cuts Pam off before she can finish. "Look here, my friend. I've got this."

"Okay, okay. Do you, girl?"

Through the window, Crystal watches a flirtatious couple cuddling. Her eyes scale the street, and she spots a large family climbing into an SUV. The sight puts a smile on Crystal's face. To draw Crystal's attention back to the conversation, Pam says. "I just have one last question. Have the two of you gone out on a date lately?"

"What's up with all the questions? He still comes over to see me."

Pam stacks and pushes her plates aside. She grabs her purse as she rises to her feet. She shakes her head as she replies, "That is not what I asked you. The once presumed good girl has become a booty call for a man who is trying to get it right with the Lord." Pam sighs. "Your best bet is to start going to church with him, or he will probably meet someone else there."

Crystal sneers at Pam as she ponders those words. She then states, "We used to have so much fun together."

The two women leave a tip on the table and walk out of the diner together. Crystal is deep in thought.

*****

Those thoughts take her back two years. In Crystal's apartment, she rushes to get dressed. Pam sits on the bed, watching Crystal prance back and forth from the closet to the mirror, and back again. Each time she is wearing a different outfit. Pam blurts out, "Don't mess this up. You have only been dating two weeks, and I can tell that he really likes you."

"Don't you think that I know that? I can handle myself, so don't worry about it."

"Okay then, let me just make it plain for you, Crystal. Don't be in a hurry to sleep with him."

"Pam, I already have a mother. I don't need two."

Crystal returns to the closet to try on different shoes with the current outfit. She has a different shoe on each foot to make the comparison as she asks Pam a question, "Now which of these shoes looks best with this dress?"

Before Pam can respond, they hear the doorbell. In excitement, Crystal chooses a pair. She shuffles across the room to get them on while stumbling out the room to answer the front door.

"Just a minute. I'm coming."

Crystal makes a final adjustment, straightening her dress and hand-grooming her hair. She then opens the front door. A very handsomely dressed Solomon stands there smiling and handing Crystal a single rose. Pam has moved from the bedroom to the living room and is watching. As Solomon hands Crystal the rose, his eyes follow her from head to toe.

"Wow, you do look nice."

Crystal takes the rose and, with an ear-to-ear smile, softly says, "Thank you."

Pam is still watching as she slowly moves closer, walking between them, and then out the front door. She looks at Solomon.

"Hey, Solomon, how's it going?"

"Hello, Pam."

Both Solomon and Crystal smile at one another as they watch Pam head down the hall. When she reaches her apartment, Pam looks back.

"Have fun, you guys, and stay out of trouble."

In response, Crystal exclaims, "Shut up, Pam."

Solomon extends his arm to Crystal. Crystal locks her door as she locks her arms with Solomon. The handsome couple walks down the hall and out of the building.

*****

Early the next morning, in Crystal's apartment, Solomon rushes to dress himself as he makes his way through the apartment and out of the front door. Crystal is following close behind. She is wearing a robe and she stops at the door. As she holds it open, she puckers up. Solomon gives her a peck on the lips and continues down the hall toward the exit.

"Why are you rushing off? I thought you didn't have to work today."

"I don't, but I do have a few errands to run. I'll call you later."

Crystal is leaning on the outer doorframe, as she nods her head okay. Startled by a noise, she turns her head in the other direction and sees Pam peeking through her apartment door. Agitated, Crystal steps inside her own apartment and slams the door.

*****

Arriving at his vehicle, Solomon stops to recollect. He looks up to see Crystal now staring out of the window at him. He smiles, waves, and then climbs in, driving off. While driving, Solomon thinks of the night before. He thinks of Crystal's embrace, her gentle kisses, and the time spent over a candlelight dinner at one of the city's finest restaurants. Soon thereafter, Solomon parks his vehicle at his own apartment complex and rushes into the building.

Moving quickly, Solomon jumps in and out of the shower, grabs a suit from the closet, then dresses himself. In a standing mirror, he adjusts and readjusts his tie. He grabs his Bible from the dresser top, rushes to the front room, stops at the door to say a silent prayer, and then exits again. He makes a mad rush for his vehicle on his way to church. Solomon arrives at church and passes the marquee at the entrance which reads, "ANNUAL CHURCH PICNIC," Saturday, July 15, 1995.

*****

Present day

The year is 1997. Solomon arrives at "House of Praise Christian Ministries." The church marquee reads, "ANNUAL CHURCH PICNIC," Saturday, July 19, 1997. Solomon finds a parking space and then enters the sanctuary, which is full. Several single ladies make eye contact with Solomon. Solomon smiles at them all as he makes his way to a seat near the front. Victoria, an attractive young woman, thirtyish is singing lead with the choir. Solomon finds a seat while studying her moves. She finishes her song and takes a seat in the choir stand. Elderly Pastor Sullivan takes his place at the podium. He begins, "I was glad when they said unto me, 'Let us go into the house of the Lord.'"

The sermon is relevant and uplifting as usual. The choir sings beautifully, and everyone scurries about with their business of the ministry as usual. That is to say, the ushers led people to their seats, the deacons led devotions, and the mothers of the church continued to keep everyone in line. Same old routine, but necessary and refreshing as always.

After the sermon, Pastor Sullivan invites sinners to join the church and come to know Jesus. Soon after the closing prayer, Solomon takes another look at Victoria who has also been watching him. He then headed out the door and to his vehicle. Once outside, Solomon stands nonchalantly by his vehicle watching the door. When Victoria steps outside, Solomon turns toward his vehicle and fiddles around with his keys to open the car door. Victoria shouts out to Solomon, "Solomon! Solomon! Wait up."

Solomon pretends to be startled as he turns around in response. "Hey, girl, what's going on?"

Victoria walks briskly toward Solomon. "You tell me, you never hang around long enough for anyone to talk to you." Victoria caresses Solomon's arm. "You're always dressed so nicely. Have you been avoiding me?'

Solomon pulls the wrinkles from his suit. Other church members start to fill the parking lot as they head home. Some stare at Solomon and Victoria and begin to point and whisper.

"Avoiding you? No, not at all. In fact, I was just going to invite you to join me for lunch."

"Really? I mean, sure. Why not."

Victoria moves to the passenger side of Solomon's vehicle, grabbing the handle. Solomon sneers and says, Umm! Drive your own car. I'll meet you there. The Café around the corner; okay?

Victoria appears disappointed. As she turns toward her own vehicle, she simply says, "Okay."

They each climb into their own vehicles and drive off. Some of the mothers of the church look on with discerning looks on their faces. One squints her eyes and, with her hands on her hips, shakes her head at Victoria as she is driving off.

At the café, in a booth, near a window, Solomon and Victoria sit across from one another. They enjoy a delicious lunch over the conversation.

"So, Solomon, why aren't you married yet?" Or am I being too nosy?"

"Seriously, you want to jump right into my business like that."

Victoria doesn't seem to have much home training. She speaks with a mouth full of food. "I'm just saying, it seems that a nice guy like you would already be settled down by now."

"I guess it's just not my time yet. How about you?"

Victoria does not realize that she looks like a mess. She has spilled gravy on her blouse and has mashed potatoes on the tip of her nose. Solomon points to the stain on her blouse. Victoria dips a napkin into her water glass. She then attempts to clean the stain. Solomon tries to refrain from laughing. While dabbing at the stain, Victoria answers Solomon's question. "Actually, I was married once."

"Oh, yeah, I didn't know that."

"You never asked me. What?"

Solomon points to his nose, indicating that Victoria should wipe hers. She wipes the potatoes from her nose. They both chuckle. Embarrassed, Victoria decides to change the subject.

"Whatever happened with the position you applied for, working the unsolved cases? Did you get it?"

"How did you hear about that?"

"You told me. Don't you remember telling me that several people had applied for the position?"

"I don't remember telling you that. However, I can't think of any reason why I wouldn't get it. I should be hearing something soon."

"Good, that position should afford you more free time, right?"

"Not necessarily. It will however be a nice change. I'm looking forward to something new and purposeful."

Solomon checks his watch and pushes his plates aside. He places a tip on the table. Victoria follows his lead and begins to gather her purse and sweater. They both stand to leave. Victoria takes ahold of Solomon's arm as they approach the exit.

"Do you think we can hook up tomorrow?"

"You really should wait for me to ask you."

"Seriously, Solomon, what difference does it make who asks?"

"I'm starting to feel like this was a mistake."

"What is that supposed to mean?"

The two reach their cars outside. Solomon gently pulls away from Victoria. He begins to feel guilty and has thoughts of Crystal.

"Look, I'm sorry if I have been misleading in any way."

"Don't be silly. What are you doing tonight?"

"You are not listening. I have other plans."

Solomon climbs into his vehicle. Victoria stands there scowling as he pulls off.

As Solomon drives off, he is deep in thought; many images appear in his mind. The images include a dead body lying in a pool of blood, a pileup of cars on an interstate with casualties, and a suicide victim with a bullet in his head. His final thought takes him back twenty-five years to the female corpse under the floorboards of the boarded-up old house.

CHAPTER

3

Later that evening, Solomon, Otis, and another younger colleague, Gus, sit at a table in a nightclub. They are enjoying drinks, snacks, and conversation. Otis addresses Gus. "Hanging out with detectives doesn't make you one. You do know that, right, Gus?"

"Trust me. I will make detective in no time."

Solomon adds, "Why not just focus on being a good cop for now."

On the dance floor, a heavyset man, in his sixties, and dressed in brightly colored clothes, dances with a woman half his age. An even younger woman close by competes for his attention. Amused by the antics of the two women, Otis points them out to Solomon.

"That's you, Solomon. Thirty years from now."

All three men burst into laughter.

"No, I don't think so."

Gus then asks Solomon, "Why not? Do you think you will have lost your swagger by then?"

Solomon does not respond right away. An altercation between the two women catches his attention. The older gentleman attempts to escort his lady from the dance floor, gently pushing the other woman aside. Gus loudly exclaims, "Look at that old fart. He actually has game."

Solomon responds, "No, that's probably his wife. He's just trying to keep the peace."

"Keep the peace? He was hoping to see a brawl."

Otis shakes his head no. "Solomon is right. If he wanted to see a fight, why would he have separated them?"

The older woman reaches back and slaps the younger woman. The younger woman looks stunned as she stands there holding the side of her face. The couple makes their way to a table and take their seats on the other side of the room. From their table, Otis, Gus, and Solomon observe the situation. Then they all burst into laughter.

Solomon continues, "That's his wife, and she is not playing. Of course, my wife would handle herself better than that. Violence is never necessary."

Otis raises an eyebrow. "Did he say *wife*?"

Gus replies, "He did. He definitely said *wife*."

Solomon wipes the sweat from his brow and retorts, "I was speaking hypothetically."

Otis then asks, "Now is that hypothetically Victoria or Crystal?"

Nervously, Solomon answers, "Crystal, I suppose. Anyhow, you sort of dig Victoria, don't you, Otis?"

"As if you didn't know. Since you knew that, why would you even take her out for lunch?"

"Yes, I heard about that."

"My bad buddy. You do know that it was just lunch, right?"

"I certainly hope so. Even though she turned me down when I asked."

Solomon checks his watch, finishes his drink, and gathers his things to leave. "That's it for me, fellas. I've got to see about a beautiful lady."

Otis and Gus look at each other and simultaneously say, "He's in love."

Solomon waves and exits the club.

*****

Just across town, on that same evening, Crystal is curled up in a chair at home, reading a book. The coffee table in front of her is covered with dirty dishes, snacks, and a television remote. The doorbell rings, surprising Crystal. She pauses for a moment as if to ponder her next move. The doorbell rings again.

"Coming, just a minute!"

Crystal tries to clean the mess in a hurry. She grabs several items and rushes into the kitchen. She attempts to organize the rest of the mess on the coffee table. She runs to the door and peeks through the hole. She opens the door. Solomon is standing there, grinning and wearing the same suit he had on at the club.

"Well, if it isn't Solomon the preacher man."

"Don't call me that."

Solomon kisses Crystal on the cheek and then heads for the sofa. He plops down on the sofa and watches as Crystal closes the door and moves closer. He asks her, "What did you cook today?"

"Catfish and spaghetti. I'll get you a plate."

"Okay, sounds good."

Solomon gets comfortable, removing his shirt, shoes, socks, and belt. He tosses them across the room and onto Crystal's cozy recliner. Solomon grabs the remote and places his feet on the coffee table. Crystal glares at Solomon from the kitchen as she prepares his plate. Solomon is flipping through channels. Crystal speaks with an attitude.

"I can't even remember the last time that we actually went out anywhere together. That's not a good thing."

Solomon retorts, "You always seemed to enjoy spending time together right here. You never complained about it before."

Crystal walks with one hand on her hip and Solomon's meal in the other. She stands in front of him while speaking with attitude once again.

"Yes, that is my point exactly." She places the plate on the table in front of him. She then takes a seat beside him. "Most of our time together has been spent here, between these four walls, and I'm tired of that. I need to get out of this house sometimes."

Solomon retorts, "What about your girl Pam? You two go out every weekend."

"No, we don't go out every weekend and quit trying to change the subject, Solomon. I'm talking about us."

Solomon grabs Crystal, holding her and tickling her until she begins to laugh.

"Let me go, Solomon. It's not funny. This is serious."

"I hear what you're saying, Crystal, and I've been thinking about some things too."

They refrain from embracing and look into each other's eyes. Crystal replies, "Yes, I'm listening."

"You are fully aware of my calling to preach. We have to start doing things by the book."

Crystal nods in agreement, and Solomon continues. "It's time for me to answer my calling. I can't keep putting it off."

"I knew that you were going to preach before you even told me. I saw it in a dream."

"Yes, well God told me in a dream long before he showed you, Crystal. For me, the question has always been when. What would be the starting point of this season change in my life?"

"Solomon, the obvious starting point is that we begin worshipping together. How about us going to church together this coming Sunday?"

"To my church?"

"Why wouldn't you want me at your church, Solomon? Is there something going on there that you don't want me to know about?"

"Not at all, Crystal. Just make sure that you're doing this for the Lord, not me. Okay?"

Crystal grabs the plate from the coffee table and heads to the kitchen to wrap it.

"You are absolutely right, Solomon. I'll wrap this so you can take it with you."

Solomon gets dressed again. Crystal returns to the living room, handing Solomon his wrapped plate. They walk to the front door together and share a gentle kiss. Solomon exits, and Crystal shuts the door behind him. She lingers there for a moment pondering their future together. She smiles.

*****

In Solomon's apartment, he awakens early the next morning. The sun is not yet up; however, he swings his feet to the floor. Grasping the edge of his bed with both hands while bowing his head, Solomon says a silent prayer. Lifting his head afterward, he looks at the nightstand beside his bed where his Bible lay open. He flips through the pages to find a passage to read for the day. Soon after he finishes his reading, the phone rings. The caller ID indicates that the call is coming from his office at work. Solomon puts the phone on speaker and begins his morning regimen to get ready for work.

"Hello, who is calling me, and why are you in my office?"

*****

Across town in the Police Headquarters, officers and staff are beginning shift change. Gus is standing near a bulletin board in the central office area where promotions have been posted. He notices "SOLOMON PHELPS" in big boldface letters. In excitement, he turns in the direction of Solomon's office. On the door in boldface print is "Detective Solomon Phelps." Gus lets himself in and rumbles through the inbox on the desk. He takes a seat in Solomon's chair. Using Solomon's office phone, he places a call.

"Solomon, it's me, Gus. I'm in your office because I wanted to confirm what I saw on the bulletin board and to be the first to congratulate you on your promotion."

"Gus, what are you talking about?"

Gus begins to talk fast. He hopes that Solomon will hear him out.

"It looks like you are going to be working cold cases now. I am looking at your promotion papers as we speak. Unsolved cases are right up my alley too. I'm just the man who can help you with that. Congratulations, man."

"So that finally came through. Thanks, and all that, but get out of my office."

Solomon's office is cluttered with labeled cold case files. The dates on the boxes vary. Gus is anxiously thumbing through them all. A secretary steps into the office carrying additional files. She appears tired, and she asks, "Are you sure Detective Phelps is okay with this? Where should I put the rest of these files?"

Overhearing the discussion, Solomon says, "What's going on over there, Gus? I know you heard me tell you to get out of my office."

Gus addresses the secretary first. "I'm sure he's fine with it. Just put them anywhere."

The secretary finds a clear spot on the floor, dropping the boxes. She then exits. Gus responds to Solomon's remarks, "Yes, Detective Phelps, I heard you. More importantly, I want to help you get started with these unsolved cases. Does any particular case or era strike your interest?"

In the mirror of his bedroom, Solomon puts the finishing touches on his business look. His thoughts take him back twenty-five years. He can see the face of the female corpse under the floorboards of the abandoned house.

"Yes. Pull all the files from 1972."

*****

Solomon leaves his apartment and rushes to his vehicle. He secures his earpiece and places a phone call. Gus is still in Solomon's office, and he picks up the telephone.

"Detective Phelps' office. Officer Leggs speaking."

"Somehow I knew you would still be there. Did you pull those files from 1972 yet?"

"I sure did, Detective. So what exactly am I looking for?"

"I will take it from there, Gus. Please be out of my office when I arrive."

Solomon ends the call and says aloud, "Lord, I'm going to need your help on this one."

Solomon drives at a slow pace as he reflects on his life. Solomon's thoughts take him to an embrace he shared with Crystal, a moment of flirting with Victoria, and a time of partying at the club, with the fellas. He reflects on reading his Bible, remembers a gruesome crime scene of multiple murders, and finally envisions himself as a preacher in the pulpit.

Solomon snaps out of his daze and finds himself in Granny's neighborhood, where he grew up. As Solomon cruises by the lot where the abandoned house once stood, he notices something on one of the pet tombstones. He stops and then backs the vehicle up for a closer look. He notices that one of the Tombstones simply says "AIMEE."

"Whoa!? That's weird."

Solomon studies the site for a moment and then pulls off.

Solomon arrives at the Police Headquarters, parks his car, and then climbs the steps to the entry. Upon entry, Solomon receives applause from his colleagues and friends. He nods in response and quickly makes his way toward his office. Once again, Bernard Burgess is present and engaged in conversation with the police chief. He and Solomon watch each other, but neither of them speaks.

Upon entering his office and shutting the door behind him, Solomon looks around. His office is full of clutter. On his desk, cabinets, and floors are numerous boxes labeled 1972 cold case files. He separates the boxes by date, stacking the ones from October through December closest together. He starts with boxes from December. He searches for the case on Aimee, hoping to find a picture or discover her full name. Suddenly, the door opens, and Otis walks in without knocking.

"Congrats, man, on getting the job you wanted. Same old dusty office though."

"Yeah, Same ole. And thanks."

Otis looks at the clutter with a look of disgust on his face. He shakes his head. "What a mess. You know you can't work them all at once."

"Yes, I know that, O. There is one that I am hoping to start with."

Otis notices that the dates of the files on Solomon's desk are from the winter of 1972. He points to the date and excitedly exclaims, "This is about that woman we found, isn't it?"

"Yes, but I've had no success yet in finding the original report."

Otis is a little nervous. He takes a seat on top of a stack of file boxes. "So if you couldn't find anything, it's probably because that case was solved years ago."

"No, O. I checked for her name in the system some time ago. Nothing solid with her picture, name, or even close if Aimee was short for something else. I figured it would be here somewhere in cold cases, misplaced. I will never forget her face."

"Okay, Solomon, maybe she was a Jane Doe, and the records got lost. It happens."

"So then I'm probably searching in the right place. These files are a mess, and sometimes these pages are sticking together. I will find out who she was and solve her case. I believe it's why I found her. God has put her on my mind for a reason."

"You definitely don't want to disappoint him, Solomon, so do your thing. Good luck with your first unsolved case."

Otis exits Solomon's office, shutting the door behind him. Solomon ponders for a moment and then speaks aloud to himself. "Who are you, Ms. Aimee?"

Solomon picks up the phone on his desk and dials a number. He holds the phone for a while, allowing it to continuously ring. He is determined to speak with his father. Finally, there is an answer.

"Williams' Auto Body. Tyrone speaking."

"Hey, Pops, I need to talk."

CHAPTER 4

In the business district of the city and in line with several private-owned businesses sits one of three Williams' Auto Body shops. Seated on a bench just outside of the main entrance is the owner. Tyrone Williams is a gray-haired seventy-year-old man who still looks fabulous for his age. Not only is he an extraordinarily successful businessman, but he has also given back to the community in numerous ways over the years. Solomon turns onto this business strip, spots his father sitting outside, and then pulls over to park in front. He smiles as he exits his car and approaches Tyrone.

"Hey, Pops, do you ever plan on retiring?"

Tyrone stands to embrace his son. "What? And leave these knuckleheads to run my shop? It's not likely."

Loud music is coming from the shop. His employees enjoy their work as they dance, work, and talk loudly among themselves. An elaborate sports car pulls toward the exit while an exchange for its services is rendered at the front desk. After exiting the sports car, the employee directs its owner to the cashier's window. The owner is overly dressed and adorned with jewelry. The employee smiles and winks at Tyrone.

"Well, Pops, you certainly don't need the money."

"No, I don't need the money. I just love what I do. Are you hungry?"

Tyrone places his arm around Solomon's shoulder, and they begin to walk down the street to the Bar and Grill. A cute hostess in her twenties greets Solomon and Tyrone at the entrance.

"Hello, Mr. Williams."

"Hey, baby, how are you today?"

She turns to grab two menus from the front podium while staring and grinning at Solomon. "I'm fine, thanks. Table for two? Smoking, right, Mr. Williams?"

"That will be fine."

Solomon scowls at Tyrone, and they both follow the hostess. They both grin and look at each other, indicating an appreciation for the swaying of her hips. Stopping at a booth, she places the menus in front of them. Solomon opens his, but Tyrone hands his back immediately. He then takes a cigarette lighter from his pocket, placing it on the table near an ashtray.

"Patty melt with slaw instead of fries. And bring me a Pepsi."

"Is Coke okay? We have Coke."

Although she is speaking to Tyrone, she is flirting with and staring at Solomon. The hostess nervously sways her body from side to side to the rhythm of the music playing softly throughout the restaurant. She begins to brush her hair behind her ears with her fingers and further says, "I'm not your server, but I will take your order for you. It's not a problem."

Solomon does not even look in her direction. He hands her the menu over his shoulder and states, "I'll have the same."

The hostess has a look of disappointment on her face. She takes the menu and walks away. A busboy begins cleaning a table nearby. He is holding a plastic container into which he wipes debris and places dirty dishes. Tyrone has a look of disappointment on his face as he speaks to Solomon. "What's up with you? That's a sweet little lady right there. She took our order just so she could talk to you."

"I didn't mean to be rude to her. I'm just not in the mood for flirting right now."

Tyrone pulls a gold cigarette case from his pocket. He takes out one and places the case on the table. He grabs his lighter from the table. As soon as he has lit it, Solomon snatches it and puts it out in the ashtray. Solomon then snatches the expensive cigarette case and tosses it into the busboy's container. Solomon then addresses the busboy. "Pretty box, bad habit. Throw that away for me, okay?"

The busboy picks up the cigarette case, admiring it. He then nods his head yes while putting it into his back pocket. Solomon stretches his arm out to place the ashtray on another table nearby. Shortly thereafter, the hostess returns with their drinks. She places their drinks in front of them and turns to walk away. Solomon grabs her hand. She turns to look in his direction. He is now sporting a huge smile.

"Thank you so much, pretty lady."

"No problem."

The hostess walks away smiling. The waiter brings their food. As they enjoy their lunch, the father and son continue their conversation. Tyrone changes the subject. "How are the renovations coming with those properties I gave you?"

"Well, Pops, with the challenges from the new position in cold cases, I really haven't had much time."

"So if it's not the properties, then what was it that you wanted to talk about?"

"There is so much going on with me right now that I'm not really sure where to start. Perhaps, I should start with Crystal. You do remember Crystal?"

Tyrone cracks a smile and listens intently.

Solomon continues, "There is something about that woman. Pops, I'm sure that she is the one, although I may have gotten a little sidetracked with Victoria."

"Victoria? Who is that?"

"It's a long story. The short version is that she and Otis make a much better couple."

"What? Son, you are doing a lot of talking, but you are not making a lot of sense. Just talk to me. Tell me what is going on with you. We have all day."

"Okay, then. I'll take you back to when I was thirteen. Do you remember my baptism?"

Tyrone and Solomon look at each other, and their thoughts take them both back several years.

*****

The year is 1977, and Pastor Sullivan baptizes the thirteen-year-old Solomon. Those present are Agnes, Granny, and on the other side of the sanctuary, Tyrone Williams. Both Pastor Sullivan and young Solomon are clothed in white. Deacon Hodges is wading in the baptismal pool also to assist with the emergence. As the pastor places his hand on the head of Solomon and prepares to dunk him, he loudly announces, "On the profession of your faith and in the presence of these witnesses, I baptize you in the name of Jesus."

There is a joyous response from the congregation.

*****

The thoughts of Tyrone and Solomon return to their present-day conversation. Still seated at the Bar and Grill, Tyrone responds, "Yes, of course, I remember that. Continue."

"It was confirmed in my spirit right then."

"What was confirmed?"

"Pops, I have a calling on my life to preach. I have known for years. I just had not really been sure about the timing. I am learning that sometimes in life, seasons can overlap. I love my work as a detective, but I'm trying to see how that and preaching are connected."

Tyrone ponders for a moment his son's words, and then submits, "I've never been much of a religious man myself, but you are a smart man, son. God has gifted you in many ways. When the time comes, you will know what to do. You also know what to do about your relationship with

Crystal. You do not need my help with that. If you need to talk, you always know where to find me."

Solomon nods as they both stand to leave. Solomon places a generous tip on the table, and they exit the Bar and Grill. Outside, the two take the walk back in the other direction toward Williams' Auto Body. After the walk, Tyrone takes a deep breath as if exhausted. He hugs Solomon, then reclaims his seat on the bench outside. Solomon walks to his car, and as he is opening the door, a car rushes by. Otis is the driver. He does not even notice Tyrone or Solomon outside of the shop. Tyrone leans forward a little to see Otis's car at the red light. He asks Solomon, "Isn't that Otis?"

Solomon turns to look before stepping into his car. "That's him."

"It's ironic that he would pass by just then. The two of you have been joined at the hip since you were babies."

Solomon chuckles, climbs into his car, and then drives off. Tyrone continues to watch the two drive off. He then stares down the street at all the private-owned businesses, reminiscing. Tyrone's thoughts take him back to the days he and Solomon had just previously discussed. He is remembering when his autobody shop, the bakery, flower shop, and others were new storefronts.

*****

The year is 1977, and Solomon and Otis tussle playfully just outside of the bakery. The vendor, Mrs. Owens, is cleaning the counter. She can see the boys from the large front window. The boys stop wrestling and then begin whispering. Solomon opens the bakery door, and they both step inside. Solomon walks up to the counter. Mrs. Owens now has her hands on her hips. Solomon asks, "Do you need someone to clean outside of your store? I will only charge a dollar."

Otis slightly pushes Solomon aside, stepping in front of him, and correcting him. "That's two dollars."

Mrs. Owens emerges from behind the counter.

"I can sweep and clean it myself for nothing. Aren't you boys supposed to be in school?"

Otis opens the door to leave. Solomon following close behind retorts, "You obviously don't have any kids, lady. School is out for summer."

Otis exclaims loud enough for Mrs. Owens to hear him. "Man! What a grump. Let's get out of here."

The boys burst into laughter as they scurry down the street. Mrs. Owens opens the door and shouts, "Solomon, I know your father, and he would not approve of this disrespect."

"Yes, ma'am. Sorry, ma'am."

"I thought so."

Mrs. Owens gives both boys a look of disapproval and then reenters the bakery. With their attitudes well adjusted, Otis and Solomon continue walking. A few doors down, at the next cross street, they see Tyrone standing in front of his shop, smoking. Solomon looks at Otis.

"Pops paid me twenty dollars once for cleaning his shop."

"For real? Twenty dollars? Then let's go."

Solomon very excitedly replies, "When we're finished cleaning up, we can play Centipede, Space Invaders, and Pac-Man."

"All right, I haven't played those games in a long time."

Tyrone looks down the street and sees the boys approaching. He drops his cigarette and steps on it. Loud noises are coming from inside of the autobody shop. It is a combination of power tools and music. Tyrone greets the boys with high fives. "Are you, guys, staying out of trouble?"

"We're trying to, Pops. Do you have some work for me and O today?"

Otis follows with, "Yeah, we're not afraid of hard work."

Tyrone holds the door open, and the boys enter. Pac Man, Space Invaders, Centipede, and other game machines line one wall. Several customers are seated in the lobby. Tyrone points the boys in the direction of full trash bags and cleaning supplies.

"The cleaning supplies are over there. Make sure that you sweep outside and inside before you mop. Don't forget to put new liners in those cans after you take the trash out."

Solomon reaches for the mop, which is in a bucket full of dirty water. Several other supplies are stacked against a window. Solomon sneers. "Yuck. It looks like no one emptied the bucket from the last cleaning."

Otis looks in the bucket and contorts his face. The boys begin working diligently to get the shop clean. Occasionally, Tyrone peeks in on the boys to make sure they are not goofing off. Otis spots him peeking and says to Solomon, "Mr. Williams is sort of like a daddy to both of us. Do you remember when he bought our entire team's peewee baseball uniforms?"

Solomon smiles and nods yes. Otis continues. "You know what else?"

"What?"

"You earned that twenty dollars he gave you because he is working us to death."

Those words tickled Tyrone. Laughing, he replies, "If you want anything in life, you better learn now that you are going to have to work for it. Would you guys like some pizza?"

Solomon answers, "Yes, Pops. That'll work."

Otis turns to Solomon. "Sounds good. Pizza and cash. He is the coolest."

"I told you."

*****

Tyrone stops reminiscing and returns to the present in his thoughts. He laughs to himself and enters his shop. He walks through the shop and into his office. Tyrone takes a seat at his desk and opens a drawer. In the drawer, he finds several old pictures. He spreads them out across his desk, studying them one at a time. The first picture is of him and his employees. The second is of Otis, Solomon, and another male child, all age eight. A third picture is of him and Aimee. The last photo is a headshot of Aimee. Aimee is the woman found dead in the abandoned house years ago. Tyrone's eyes begin to tear as he studies her photograph.

Tyrone slides back deep into his seat and stares in deep thought.

*****

Tyrone is reminiscing again. The year is 1977 when teen boys Solomon and Otis loved a good game of basketball. On one day, after defeating a few friends, they began walking from the park and toward Williams' Auto Body. Other boys yell insults from the park toward the winners. Solomon continues to dribble the lifeless ball and ignores the remarks. Otis watches Solomon. "That ball has definitely seen better days."

"Yes, but do you realize how many games we won with this ball? I might have to retire it now though."

"You can't do that, Solomon. Let's see if we can reinflate it at Mr. Williams' shop."

Otis snatches the ball from Solomon. Solomon snatches it back. "No, it's worn and time to put it to rest. I'm definitely going to keep it though."

"Man! Now we'll have to use my ball."

Solomon shakes his head at Otis. As the boys draw closer, they see Tyrone outside. He is talking with a customer. The customer gets into his vehicle and drives off. Tyrone asks the boys, "Is that the same ball I gave you years ago?"

Solomon answers, "It sure is, Pops. It won its last game today though. Do you have some Pepsi in there?"

"There should be some in the refrigerator. While you are in there, clean up the lobby and my office."

Tyrone remains outside to greet customers approaching. Solomon and Otis rush in, heading for the refrigerator. Tyrone enters the shop shortly thereafter, checking on his workers. Solomon and Otis grab Pepsis from the refrigerator, which is alongside the office door entrance. They tussle and have not yet begun working. Tyrone spots the boys goofing off.

"Hey! Hey! Solomon!"

"Yeah, Pops."

"File those receipts on my desk in chronological order."

Otis has a confused look on his face. He asks, "Krono who? Is he going to pay us?"

The boys enter the office and look around. The office is in disarray. Solomon takes a seat at the desk and begins filing the receipts. "Let's just do it this time. Don't even ask to be paid."

"Man, you must be crazy. I need some cash."

Solomon just snickers but continues filing. Otis begins to sweep. They continue to clean for several hours. Once finished, Solomon reclines in the chair with his feet on the desk and hands behind his head. Otis leaves the office and returns shortly thereafter with two Pepsis. He hands one to Solomon.

Otis stacks two containers on the floor and takes a seat. They relax for a moment. Tyrone enters with various sports equipment, including a new basketball. The boys are excited. Tyrone places everything on the floor and asks,

"Do you think this is enough to keep you guys out of trouble for a while?"

CHAPTER 5

Present day, 1997

Ernestine Phelps (aka Granny) is sitting on the front porch of her home. She can see Solomon's vehicle making a turn onto her street. There is no room to park, so Solomon pulls into Granny's driveway. Solomon exits his car and waves at Granny. He then continues walking down the street toward the makeshift pet graveyard. Granny rises, grabs the rail around the porch, and leans in.

"Hey, baby. Where are you going? I thought you were coming to see me."

"In a minute, Granny. I'm on the job right now." Solomon pauses and turns toward Granny. "Is my mother at home?"

"Is she ever?"

Solomon shakes his head and continues down the street. Granny has a look of disappointment on her face. She puts her hands on her hips and hollers to Solomon.

"What kind of detective work would have you here on our street?"

Solomon does not respond. He enters the lot and studies the area around the marker "AIMEE." There are various discarded old containers, tools, furniture, and rubbish throughout the tiny graveyard. Solomon finds an old shovel and begins digging. Suddenly, he hears a familiar voice calling his name.

"Solomon, Solomon."

Solomon turns to see his mother, Agnes, standing on the sidewalk, just outside of the lot. He is a little unhappy about being interrupted. He hesitates, drops the shovel, and then joins Agnes on the sidewalk.

"Mom, you are one hard woman to catch up with."

"Give your momma a hug. Let's walk down here to see Granny."

Solomon gives his mother a warm embrace. They walk arm in arm to Granny's house.

Granny clasps her hands together, sports a huge grin, and starts ranting.

"You may as well come on. I have been cooking all day. You're going to think it is Thanksgiving Day in here when you see all that I have cooked. Stop dragging your feet."

"Alright, Granny, but I can only stay for a couple of hours. I have to be back at the station soon."

*****

Later that day at Police Headquarters, Solomon enters the central office area, and there is loud conversation and laughter. Officer Gus is in civilian clothes and on a crutch. Solomon looks around the room.

"What's so funny? What's going on?"

A plainclothes detective answers from his desk.

"Everyone, look at Officer Gus Leggs. He'll do anything to get light duty."

Gus limps across the room on a crutch and bandaged foot, finding a seat on the edge of a desk. He lifts his foot and points out the injury. The plainclothes detective continues. "He just wants to play detective. There are no shortcuts, Leggs. You must pay your dues like everyone else."

Gus retorts, "You are the one that ran over my foot."

"He paid me."

Solomon finds humor in the whole ordeal. As he continues to his office, he stops at the door and, looking back, submits, "I believe it. He has also been operating under an alias. Isn't that right, Gus?"

Otis is at the coffee machine when he adds. "It's true. I remember when he first completed his application. I saw his real name, and he made me promise not to tell."

Solomon, now holding his door open adds, "Go ahead, Officer Leggs. Tell them what your first name really is."

Gus gets a little cozier on the desk, and, folding his arms, he answers. "It's no big deal, really. I was named after my maternal grandfather."

The plainclothes officer asks again, "So, Officer Leggs, what is your first name?"

Gus replies, "Harry."

Everyone bursts into laughter. Solomon notices a scruffy, unkempt, gray-haired Melvin Grady, (Tyrone's hanging Buddy from back in the day), sitting near a detective's desk. He is in handcuffs and a detective questions him. Melvin lifts his head and, upon seeing Solomon, drops it again. Solomon addresses Melvin. "Melvin, how is Mrs. Grady?"

Melvin shrugs his shoulders but does not say a word. Just before entering his office, Solomon moves in closer to the bulletin board. Posted are the usual numerous photographs of missing persons. Although he had never seen it there before, Solomon finds a photograph of Aimee. The corner of the picture has a fresh tear on it. He whispers to himself, "This couldn't have been here all this time."

He takes the picture and enters his office, shutting the door behind him. On his desk is an absolute mess from the previous search for Ms. Aimee's identity. He began the search again. He could not remember if one of the files was missing a photograph. All the files in his office now are from 1972. Solomon takes his seat at his desk. He ponders over this photograph, has a flashback remembrance of the woman under the floorboards, and now can even remember her familiar face from the past. It occurs to him at this moment that he had seen her before. She had been a regular customer at Williams' Autobody Shop. Surely, she was someone that Tyrone knew well.

Solomon continues the tedious task of searching numerous files again in hopes of discovering Aimee's identity. Then suddenly, one file stands out. This file is missing a photograph. A corner of a torn picture is stapled to the file folder. Solomon lines up Aimee's photo against the tear and finds it to be a perfect fit. A closer examination of the folder's contents shows the missing person's name to be Amelia Williams, aka Aimee. The person filing the report,

Tyrone Williams. Solomon is shocked to discover that Ms. Aimee is his half sister.

Otis abruptly walks in without knocking. He sees the look on Solomon's face. "Are you okay? Is this job wearing you out already?"

Solomon tucks the photograph away and reclines in his chair. "I could use a day off, that's all."

"Well, I can understand that. The church picnic is Saturday. Are you going?"

"I'll probably be there. How about you, Otis?"

"Victoria invited me."

"Oh yes, I always thought you two would make a good couple."

"We do, don't we? So stop flirting with her, Solomon. It can be misleading you know."

"You're right. My bad. I'll see you there."

"For sure. See you tomorrow."

Otis exits, shutting the door behind him. Solomon pulls Aimee's picture out and studies it while gazing out of his window.

CHAPTER 6

Early Saturday morning, at the city park, there is a large gathering of people for the church picnic. Solomon converses with Pastor Sullivan. Initially, Pastor is doing most of the talking.

"Are you about ready to finally answer your call? You know we can really use you in the ministry. I'm getting old, and you can stand in for me sometimes. Time to get your feet wet."

"Pastor, the first time I actually heard that calling loud and clear for myself, I was about thirteen years old. I had a dream in which I was the age I am now." Solomon shares his dream with Pastor Sullivan.

*****

Solomon is thirty-three and climbing a tall mountain. Many people are at the base of this mountain and calling out to him. Solomon looks down. He can clearly see the faces of people that he would meet later in life. Crystal hollers out to Solomon, "Solomon, why are you rushing off?"

Agnes requests, "Don't forget about your momma."

Otis asks, "Is this about that woman we found when we were kids?"

Tyrone shouts, "When the time comes, you'll know what to do."

Granny reassures with, "When the Lord has something for you to do, trust me, He will make it clear. His sheep hear his voice."

Then Solomon hears a voice like the sound of thunder coming from above the mountain. He looks up.

"Solomon! Solomon! Your work is not yet done."

A thirteen-year-old Solomon awakens from this dream. Perplexed, he sits up in bed. Still in his pajamas, he goes to the kitchen and takes a seat. Granny is already preparing his breakfast at the stove. She prepares a plate and places it in front of Solomon. After getting one for herself, she takes a seat at the table with Solomon. He shares his dream with Granny.

"Granny, I dreamed that I was older. There were a lot of people in my dream who seemed familiar although I have never met them. Is God trying to tell me something?"

"When the Lord has something for you to do, trust me, He will make it clear. His sheep hear his voice."

"That is exactly what you said in my dream."

Granny smiles and nods her head yes. Solomon continues to share the entire dream with Granny.

*****

Present day at the church picnic

Solomon continues his conversation with Pastor Sullivan.

"I'm not sure if I'm running from my calling or waiting for the right time to answer it."

"You already know the answer to that. Now, what are you going to do about it?"

About ten yards away, Solomon spots Victoria serving meals to the elderly members. She smiles and waves at the two gentlemen.

"That had been my weakness right there. For many years."

"Victoria?"

"Not specifically, just women in general."

"I know that God showed you your wife a long time ago. Although I have not seen her around here in a while. It's time to do right by her as well. Seek the Lord on that and follow your heart, my brother."

Pastor Sullivan pats Solomon on the back and walks away. Pastor Sullivan focuses his attention on another member of his congregation.

"Brother, let me talk to you for a minute."

Solomon turns and walks toward Victoria. They meet somewhere in the middle and share a brief embrace. Victoria starts the conversation.

"Deacon Hodges sure can cook some ribs."

"Yes, he can. I finished a whole slab myself."

"Dang!"

"So what about you, Victoria? Can you cook?"

"Yes, I can cook. You're still cooking for yourself though, right?"

"Granny taught me, and I'm pretty good if I do say so myself."

Otis is seated at a picnic table nearby. Otis has stacked his plate with ribs. Solomon spots Otis, who is stuffing his face with food while sneering at Solomon and making quite a mess with the barbeque sauce. It is all over his face and spilled on his shirt.

Victoria's eyes follow Solomon's stare to Otis. He waves at Victoria. She waves back. She and Solomon both look at each other and burst into laughter at his mess. Their conversation continues.

"Yes, I am quite independent. Thanks to Granny and Pops, of course."

"Speaking of independence, I finally got my license in cosmetology."

"Well, congratulations. That is fantastic. Does Otis know?"

"I haven't told anyone else yet. Why are you asking me about Otis? What's so funny?"

They both see Otis approaching. He is clearly a mess with food stains on his shirt and barbeque sauce on his face. Victoria tries to stifle her laughter.

"He is rather cute though."

"I knew it. You guys are into each other, aren't you?"

"No, nothing like that. I mean, he is your best friend."

"Yeah. So?"

"He's always alone and that's why I invited him."

"You don't have to explain anything to me. If you are feeling O, it's cool. It's not like you and I ever—"

Victoria interrupts, "And it's not like we ever could, Solomon. I'm a good girl."

As Otis approaches the two, he extends his hand. Solomon grabs his hand.

"What's up, O? I will let the two of you talk. I have to get a plate for Granny."

Solomon walks off. Victoria and Otis stand there looking at one another. They both appear to be uncomfortable.

*****

Later that evening, Solomon arrives at Granny's house carrying a foil-covered plate. He steps inside, walks through the front room, and follows the sound of the television to the kitchen. There is a small television on the kitchen countertop. Granny has taken a seat at the kitchen table, watching the television. She has a cup of hot tea in front of her.

"Hey, Granny, I brought you a plate."

"Thanks for thinking of me, baby."

"Are you feeling any better?"

Granny emerges, snatching the plate, ripping the foil, and taking her seat again. "Oh, yes, a lot better. These ribs sure look good."

Solomon takes a seat at the table with Granny to start a conversation about Agnes. Granny, fully aware of who he is looking for starts, "Agnes isn't here. She is out ripping and running as usual. I expect her home soon though."

"Awesome, I really need to talk to her. She would not let me get a word in edgewise the last time."

"That's your momma. She always did have the gift of gab. You hardly ever have time for me anymore."

"Granny, you know that is not true. I brought you that plate, didn't I?"

"Yes, but I had to be sick to get that."

"Granny, you know you need to quit."

Granny bursts into laughter and then changes the subject. "I saw your father the other day. If it were not for his gray hair, you would never even know that man is as old as I am."

Solomon stops to consider his words before speaking. "Why didn't you tell me that Mr. Williams was my father? You and Mom kept that a secret from me for years."

"That was Agnes's idea. You were always smart though. You knew Tyrone was your daddy before anyone told you. Did anyone ever tell you the story about how Tyrone and Agnes met for the first time?"

Solomon shakes his head no and listens intently.

CHAPTER 7

The year is 1963. Two voluptuous cuties, Agnes Phelps and Ruby Easton, both in their early twenties, are playing pool at the local Bar and Grill. Both ladies' apparel is seductive. Ruby is holding her pool stick while Agnes prepares to shoot. Ruby spots Tyrone on the opposite side of the room. Tyrone is fortyish, with slightly graying hair. He is handsome and very sharply dressed. He and his friend Melvin Grady have seats at a small tabletop. Both are scoping out the ladies in the building.

Ruby whispers to Agnes, "There he is, the most attractive, richest, and eligible man on this side of the Mississippi. Agnes, how old do you think he is?"

Agnes stops shooting and stands straight up, trying to get a better look. "Are you talking about Melvin or his friend?"

"Now you know I'm not talking about that wife-beater Melvin. You know she left him again. Either that, or maybe she's dead."

"Ruby, that's all speculation. How bad could he be if he has friends like Tyrone? In answering your question, he is forty or fifty. Who cares? He's fine, and besides, he's got loot."

"Agnes, that's all you care about anyway, money."

"Not so, Ruby. I also want to be happy. The money will certainly help."

They both laugh.

Ruby flirts with Tyrone, winking, waving, and blowing kisses. "I wonder if he truly is available. Just because we don't see him with anyone doesn't mean that he doesn't have a woman."

"You better hear this girl. That man over there is going to be mine. Him and everything he owns. So stop flirting with him."

"Well, all right then. Do your thing girl."

Ruby takes her turn shooting pool while Agnes makes eye contact with Tyrone.

At a small table across the room, Tyrone and Melvin talk about the women in the bar. Melvin catches Agnes flirting with Tyrone from across the room. He warns Tyrone.

"I heard about that one. She talks too much, makes you want to slap her around a bit. Do you know what I mean?"

"Seriously, Melvin, you need to deal with that issue. You should never find cause to strike a woman. If you don't learn anything else from me, learn that."

"All right, Tyrone, but I also heard that she would do anything for a dollar. She's a gold digger, man."

"Maybe so, but she's not half bad looking, and besides, our options are few tonight."

Tyrone and Melvin laugh as Tyrone rises from his seat, pulls the wrinkles from his suit, and makes his way over to Agnes. Ruby is still shooting pool, but Agnes takes a seat at a nearby table and waits for Tyrone. Melvin grabs Tyrone by the sleeve, and while snickering, he whispers, "Look, man, maybe you should leave now. You've had a little too much to drink."

Tyrone pulls away and continues walking toward Agnes's table.

"Trust me, Melvin, this is just a one-nighter."

*****

In Granny's kitchen, she is finishing the barbeque that Solomon brought her. Solomon shakes his head in disgust about the story Granny just shared with him. Granny shrugs her shoulders. "It's sad, but it's true. If she had played her cards right, she could have had a good man."

"He is a good man, Granny." Solomon checks his watch. "What time were you expecting Momma?"

"Actually, about an hour ago. You know how she is though, always late."

Frustrated, Solomon stands and heads out of the kitchen and to the front room, opening the door.

"Are you leaving, baby?"

"Yes, Granny, I have to get going. I'm having a dinner party next week to celebrate my promotion. Will you and Momma be there?"

Granny moves to the front room to see Solomon out.

"You know I don't get out much, and Agnes, who's to say. But congratulations on your promotion, honey."

"Thanks, Granny. I'll see you later."

*****

The celebration for Solomon's new position is off to a great start. Present in Solomon's apartment are Crystal, Tyrone, Gus and his date, Otis and his date, and a few others from the office. Solomon is standing at the breakfast bar peering in on his guests while preparing a tray of hors d`oeuvres. Gus, as always, is very chatty.

"Well, Solomon, you have a gravy job now. You can get away with doing absolutely nothing and nobody would even notice."

Solomon enters the room with a tray of hors d'oeuvres, placing them on the table.

"Not so, there are too many unanswered questions when it comes to unsolved cases."

Otis plants himself near the food. He begins stuffing his face and speaking at the same time.

"Yes, but, at some point, I'm sure people just want to get on with their lives. I would."

Tyrone responds, "Just because they stop talking about it certainly doesn't mean that they have let it go. It's not easy to get back to normal when you don't know what happened to someone you love."

Solomon cuddles up with Crystal, and they slowly move to the soft-playing music. He stops for a moment to add. "That's true. I received a call the other day on a case more than thirty years old."

Tyrone says, "They need answers, justice, and closure."

"Yes, Pops, and that is why I took this job. Every unsolved case deserves a second look. I'm definitely up for the challenge."

The telephone is ringing. Solomon goes into the kitchen. He lifts the phone, which is hanging on the wall. Holding the phone, while leaning against the wall, Solomon makes eye contact with Crystal. She is standing with arms folded in the spot where they were dancing.

On the phone with Solomon is Victoria. She parks on the street near the city's shopping center. Solomon answers the phone in his kitchen.

"Hello."

"Guess who?"

"Hey, Victoria. What's going on?"

Victoria is primping in the rearview mirror. Music plays loudly, and she attempts to talk over it.

"I'm just getting off work. I thought that if you weren't doing anything, maybe we could catch a movie or something."

"What? I don't get you, Victoria."

"What is that supposed to mean?"

"I thought you and Otis were talking."

"What!"

"Turn down your radio so you can hear me."

Crystal makes eye contact with Solomon as she approaches from the living room.

Victoria asks, "What were you saying about Otis?"

Crystal covers Solomon's face with kisses. Solomon continues his phone conversation.

"He's here with some random date when I know he really likes you."

"Well, he did invite me, but I thought that would be awkward since you and I dated."

Crystal is curious about the conversation. She makes a small plate of hors d'oeuvres and begins feeding Solomon. She cuddles up with Solomon trying to draw his attention away from the phone.

"Victoria, it was just lunch. You have the wrong idea about us."

"I do?"

Crystal holds Solomon's face in her hands and turns it toward her.

"Hang up the phone. There's a party going on."

Victoria hears Crystal's voice and asks questions. "Oh, you have company. Who is that?"

"Crystal, and I don't want to keep her waiting."

Crystal grabs the phone, hanging it up. Solomon returns her affection.

*****

Still seated in her car and looking at her phone with a look of disappointment on her face, Victoria dials her mother's number.

Victoria's mother is at home in her high-rise apartment. She sits on a stool, near a window that overlooks the downtown area. There is a canvas in front of her. She has painted the silhouettes of a couple embracing. She reaches for the phone lying on a nearby small table.

"Hello."

A whimpering Victoria responds, "Hey, Mom."

"Victoria, what's wrong?"

"Solomon has some woman at his house right now, and it sounds like a party is going on. He didn't even invite me."

"Well, he couldn't have both of you there now, could he?"

"That's not even funny. I'm serious."

"Have the two of you ever discussed commitment?"

"I thought it was just sort of understood."

"Apparently not. Quit running after him. Let him pursue you."

"And if he doesn't?"

"You'll survive. You want to be loved, not tolerated."

Victoria observes an elderly couple walking arm in arm. Standing in line for theater tickets is a young couple. They tussle playfully together. Victoria envies what she sees and continues her phone conversation. "I was hoping Solomon was the one."

"Don't call him again. Wait to see what he does."

"Okay, Mom. I love you."

Mom and daughter both hang up. Through her highrise window, Mom gazes at the city night lights and the illuminated sign above the theater. Victoria exits her car to stand in the ticket line. She leans against the ticket booth and sighs. She makes her request of the salesperson.

"One ticket please."

"Which movie, ma'am?"

"Whichever is the funniest. I can use some cheering up."

*****

Back at Solomon's apartment, all the dinner guests are leaving, except for Tyrone. Solomon shows them all out and then joins Tyrone on the balcony. Tyrone appears to be a little distraught as he holds on to the rail and stares into the dark of the night. Solomon addresses Tyrone, "Well, they have all gone home."

"I thought you would've taken Crystal home."

"She drove." Solomon hesitates for a moment and then asks, "Pops, why didn't you tell me about my sister?"

Tyrone turns around slowly to face Solomon. "You were so young then. I had every intention of introducing you one day, and then she came up missing. It's all my fault."

"What's your fault?"

"All I ever wanted was the best for both of you. Have you found her? Do you know what happened to her?"

"Pops, start by telling me what you remember about the last day that you saw her."

CHAPTER 8

It is a cold winter day and only a few weeks before Christmas 1972. A beautiful twenty-year-old, Amelia Williams, aka Aimee, is going from room to room in her home. She is obviously searching for something. She is dressed in a pair of slacks, with a matching vest. The blouse underneath has a checkered pattern and ties at the neck. It is her work uniform. In a heated discussion, her father, Tyrone, follows close behind.

"I thought we agreed that you would finish school first, and then we would talk about the condo."

"Daddy, that was your idea. It was more of an ultimatum for me."

"Do you mean to tell me that you would rather manage a fast-food restaurant than finish school?"

"It's not fast food. You know that it's very upscale. Besides, they're sending me to school."

"They're sending you? What about the business degree I've been paying for?"

Aimee enters the laundry room. She kneels in a pile of dirty clothes, tossing them. Tyrone stops and stands at the entryway. The conversation continues.

"Aimee, please tell me that you are not going to throw all of that away."

"It's my life, Daddy, and this is what I want to do with it."

Aimee has finished searching that pile of clothes and moves to another on the floor. Thinking aloud, she blurts, "Where is it?"

"Just take a little more time to think things over. That's all I'm asking."

"I've already done that. I just need to be on my own, so you can stop treating me like a child."

Aimee finds what she is looking for. It is a name tag with "AIMEE" engraved on it. It is attached to a vest identical to the one she is wearing.

"Here it is. Finally."

Aimee removes the name tag and secures it to the vest she is wearing. Aimee stands and rushes toward the front door. Along the way, she grabs her coat, purse, and keys. While putting her coat on, Aimee continues. "I'm taking control of my own life, starting now. That's really the end of the discussion."

"End of discussion? I'm still your father, and you still live in my house."

Stepping outside unto the porch, Aimee responds, "Not for long."

Snow covers the tops of all the homes and most of the street. The sun is going down. Aimee's cute little lime-green sports car is parked in the driveway. Suddenly, she notices a flat tire.

"Seriously, now what?"

"I can take you to work."

Aimee steps off the porch and begins her walk down the street. "That's okay, I'll catch the bus."

"Call me when you get there."

Aimee waves without looking back.

*****

Present day

In Solomon's apartment, the conversation between him and Tyrone continues. With tears in his eyes, Tyrone explains, "That was the last time I saw her. A couple of days passed, and I had not seen or heard from her. At first, I didn't think much of it."

"When did you finally realize that something was wrong?"

"Her boss kept calling. If she was not showing up for work, something had to be wrong."

"Don't worry. I promise you that I will find out what happened."

"So, you don't think that she's—"

Before Tyrone can finish his question, he can see that Solomon is nodding yes. Realizing that his daughter is dead, Tyrone collapses into Solomon's arms.

*****

Early the next day, Solomon is in his office at his desk. On his desk lay a notepad, pen, and missing person's file.

Attached to it is the photograph of Aimee. Otis walks in again without knocking.

"You know, Solomon, it really makes no sense for you to leave me voice messages when we see each other every day and work in the same office."

"It's the only way I can get a word in edgewise without being interrupted. Check this out."

Solomon removes Aimee's picture, handing it to Otis. Otis studies the picture and asks.

"Is this that woman we found? I cannot believe that case has been sitting here waiting for you all these years. Are you absolutely sure this is her?"

"Yes, it's the same woman. Her name is Amelia Williams, Aimee for short. Otis, she is my sister."

"WHAT!"

Solomon stands and hands the file to Otis. He then opens the door. "Let's take a ride. I want to show you something."

Otis and Solomon walk through the main lobby and out to their luxury cruiser.

Once they pull off, Otis opens the file and begins reading. They share a quiet ride, with Solomon in deep thought and Otis studying the report. After some time, Solomon wrinkles his nose and, with a perplexed look on his face, turns to Otis. Otis returns his stare with a smirk. Otis retorts, "What's wrong with you?"

"Did you just fart?"

"Well, yeah, I tried to hold it, but it got away from me."

Solomon lets all the windows down.

"If this wasn't so important, you would be walking right now."

Otis tries unsuccessfully to stifle his laughter. Solomon turns his car down the street that he grew up on. He drives right past Granny's house until he is directly in front of the vacant lot. Otis follows Solomon until they are standing in front of the grave marker, "AIMEE." He asks Otis, "Aimee? In this lot? Do you think it's just a coincidence?"

"It's probably just a cat. What are you doing?"

Solomon recovers the old shovel and begins digging where he left off days earlier.

"I'm making sure that this is just a cat. Aren't you even curious? I tried to get Momma and Granny to talk about this the other day. Somehow we always end up on another subject."

"Well, do either of them know that you're investigating this case?"

"No, not yet. You know how much they like to talk."

Otis is moving around anxiously with his arms folded. "That's true. Mrs. Agnes and my mother were two gossips. Mrs. Ruby Easton. Even saying my mother's name makes me emotional. I miss her. Do you really think they will know anything that would be helpful?"

"I'm not sure. However, they were the only ones we told about it. Whatever they may have learned afterward could be vital information in solving this case. Did Mrs. Ruby ever mention Ms. Aimee to you?"

Otis stops pacing and looks squarely at Solomon. "I have something to tell you, but first let me say, some things are better left unsaid. On her deathbed, my mother told me something that I would rather not have known."

*****

The year was 1979, and Ms. Ruby lie on her deathbed. She was about to end her fight with cancer. Her teenaged son, Otis, sat teary-eyed at her side. Ruby reached out with one hand, grabbing Otis by the wrist.

"Come closer, son. There is something that I must tell you. I will not take this to my grave. That just wouldn't be right."

"Mom, you should just try to get some rest."

Ruby pulls herself up and tugs at Otis to pull him yet closer. She begins, "I tried my best to be a good mother for you. I really tried to be a decent person."

"What are you trying to say, Mom?"

"Remember when you and Solomon found that dead body?"

"Mom, you are scaring me."

"Shh! Just listen, boy."

*****

It was 1972, in the middle of winter. Ruby and Agnes are sitting on the porch of Granny's house. Both bundled in outer garments, they enjoy a hot cup of cocoa over girl talk. They are appreciating the beautiful Christmas decorations on their block. Neighbors began to turn up the lights for the evening. While visually scaling the block for the best decorations, Agnes notices Amelia Williams walking down the sidewalk. She seems to be in a hurry. Getting Ruby's attention, Agnes blurts out.

"Well look who's coming on foot. Why isn't she driving that fancy little car of hers?"

"Agnes, why are you hating on that girl? She's too young to be interested in any old fart that might talk to you."

"That's not what this is about. I hope you are not suggesting that I am jealous."

"Then what do you have against her Agnes?"

"I thought you knew, that's Tyrone's daughter."

"Your baby's daddy Tyrone?"

"That's the one."

They both lean forward to get a better look at Aimee. Aimee crosses the street from one block and onto Granny's block. As she steps onto the curb, just in front of the abandoned house, she drops her purse. The contents scatter everywhere, and she quickly begins to gather them.

Ruby says to Agnes, "Well, I suppose he could have some older children. He was old when you met him. Still, that is not a reasonable excuse for hating her."

"I bet he has more children than that, which he is not even aware of. He has always been a player. Why does she get everything and my baby gets nothing?"

"Come on now, Agnes, at least the man pays child support. He would probably spend time with Solomon if you would let him."

"Still, that's not enough."

"Are you sure you're talking about Solomon and not yourself?"

Offended by that question, Agnes turns her lip up and rolls her eyes at Ruby. Ruby puts her mug down and steps off the porch. "At least you know who your child's father is. I'm not proud to say that I don't."

Ruby rushes down the stairs, out the gate, and across the street to her home.

Agnes has moved in closer and stands at the gate entry. "Ruby, why are you leaving so soon?

Looking back, Ruby replies, "I have to check on my cornbread. I could burn my house down fooling with you. I have some collards slow cooking too. I'll bring you some."

*****

Present day

Otis and Solomon stand in the lot in front of the marker "AIMEE" as Otis finishes sharing what he knows about Aimee.

"My mother told me that the next time she saw that girl, she was dead. That's all I know."

Overwhelmed by what he just heard, Solomon turns his back to Otis, looking toward Granny's house. Otis intently watches Solomon.

Without looking at Otis, Solomon says, "All this time, you could have told me about my sister."

"I didn't actually know that she was your sister."

Granny steps outside and takes a seat on her front porch. Solomon hollers out.

"Granny!"

Granny turns to see who is calling her.

"Granny, is Momma at home?"

"No, she caught a Greyhound bus this morning. She won't be home for a couple of days. She went to the casinos."

"That figures. When Momma gets home, would you have her to call me? Tie her up if you must. I really need to talk to her. I'll see you later, Granny."

Granny bursts into laughter. Solomon shakes his head and climbs into his vehicle. Otis follows Solomon, and they take a quiet drive back to Police Headquarters. Solomon drops Otis off. Otis asks, "Aren't you coming in?"

"I'll catch up with you later. I have to clear my head on some things."

Otis watches Solomon as he drives off and out of sight. Solomon drives to his apartment. He is trying to suppress his emotions. He does not acknowledge individuals who say hello when they walk by. Solomon focuses straight ahead, briskly walking until he reaches his apartment door. He opens the door and enters, slamming it behind him.

Upon entry into his apartment, Solomon drops to the floor. He begins to cry, lifting his hands up in total surrender.

"Oh, God, help me. Lord, please show me what I need to do."

Solomon is on the floor in a kneeling position, with his eyes closed. He reflects on the people in his life. He recalls his mother in a party dress, having a good time as always. There are images of Granny at worship service, He and Otis on the job and in the field, Tyrone at his shop, he and Crystal on dates, Victoria singing in the choir, and lastly, Aimee under the floorboards. Exhausted by the expectations of others and an uncertainty of where to start, Solomon prays aloud.

"Heavenly Father, your word says that the truth will set us free. I need your guidance to find the truth."

Solomon fasts that night and spends the evening studying his Bible and seeking God's face.

CHAPTER 9

Two days later, Tyrone, Otis, and Solomon all meet at the Bar and Grill for lunch. They are on one of Otis's favorite subjects—women. Although Otis cannot seem to maintain a steady relationship, he has not given up hope. In the restaurant, there is a conservatively dressed young woman, sitting alone in a booth. Solomon points her out to Otis.

"That one right there. From appearances only, I would say that she has wife potential."

Otis retorts, "Oh, yeah? Then why is she in here all alone?"

"Maybe she just wanted to go out to get some lunch. What's wrong with that?"

"I'm just saying she's probably looking for something, or should I say someone?"

"You're single, O. When you're out alone, is it always because you're looking for someone?"

"As a matter of fact, yes."

Otis snickers while stuffing his face. A woman in a skimpy blue dress takes the long route to the restroom. As she passes their table, she smiles at Tyrone. Tyrone is not talking and seems to be somewhere else in his thoughts. To draw Tyrone's attention to the conversation, Otis asks him, "Mr. Williams, what is your opinion of the lady sitting alone over there?"

Tyrone answers, "Just having lunch. Now that other one headed this way—"

The lady in the blue dress heads to her table. She passes their table again and then takes a seat with other female friends. She continues to flirt with Tyrone as she looks in his direction while pulling the wrinkles out of her hosiery, starting at the ankle.

"—in the blue dress. She is looking for attention. She has pranced back and forth across this floor several times already."

Otis responds, "You noticed that too? Mr. Williams, I hear you used to be a real ladies' man back in the day. Is that true? Were you a player, player?"

Tyrone laughs although he is a bit uncomfortable with the question. Coming to Agnes's defense, Solomon challenges Otis, "Watch it, O. What are you implying about my mother?"

Tyrone is still a bit on edge. He pulls a pack of cigarettes from his jacket's inner pocket. Before he can light it, Solomon snatches it away. Tyrone turns to Otis and says, "I knew your mother quite well, too."

"What do you mean you knew my mother?"

There is a moment of silence at their table. The three men exchange glances before bursting into laughter. Tyrone shares a story from back in the day.

*****

More than thirty years ago, indeed Tyrone was the man. At the local nightclub, Tyrone dances with several women at one time. Other women flirt with Tyrone throughout the club. Meanwhile, back in the neighborhood, Ruby is dressed to party. She rushes across the street to Granny's house and anxiously pounds on the door. She yells while pounding, "Come on, Agnes. The party is jumping right now, and you're poking around."

Agnes opens the door. Her hair is in rollers, and in the background is the sound of the television playing loudly.

Granny yells from the back room, "Agnes, you are missing *The Jeffersons*."

Ruby looks disappointed. She asks Agnes, "Why aren't you dressed yet?"

"Girl, I'm not going anywhere tonight. I have been sick all day. You go on. Just don't do anything that I wouldn't do."

Ruby starts fluffing her hair and, in jubilant response says, "Are you for real? You really aren't going tonight?"

"No, I'm not, but you don't have to be so happy about it."

"Not at all, Agnes. You know that I can have enough fun for both of us. I better be going now then. I don't want to miss my bus."

Ruby rushes down the steps and up the street. On the bus, Ruby sits up front close to a window so she can keep watch out for handsome gentlemen, especially Tyrone. She had always had as much a crush on him as Agnes did. She had hoped this would be her opportunity to get acquainted.

When the bus finally pulls over on the opposite side of the street, across from the club, Ruby exits.

She stands at the curb for a moment to fluff her hair again, while pulling the wrinkles out of her dress. Men passing by on foot as well as in cars whistle and blow their horns. Ruby spots a much younger and very sharply dressed Tyrone standing near the club's entrance. As usual, women surround him. He can see Ruby approaching from across the street. Ruby whispers to herself, "Tyrone, you are all mine tonight."

Ruby waves at Tyrone as she crosses through the middle of a busy street. Once on the other side, she pushes through the crowd and wraps her arms around Tyrone.

"Hey, Tyrone. How have you been?"

*****

Present day

Back at the Bar and Grill, Tyrone, Otis, and Solomon continue their conversation. Otis cuts Tyrone's story short. "So what are you trying to say? My mom was not a floozy."

"That's not what I meant to imply, Otis."

Solomon interjects, "There is no way that this man is my brother."

All three men laugh about it. Tyrone seems uncertain. After lunch, Otis and Solomon walk Pop Williams down to the autobody shop and climb into their cars.

*****

Solomon and Otis arrive at the station to finish the workday. Four hours later, Solomon and Otis head for home. As they exit the building and down the stairs, Otis initiates a conversation.

"I definitely earned my pay today."

"Until just now, I assumed you earned your keep every day."

Solomon is moving briskly, and Otis is trying to keep up.

"Very funny. You know what I am saying. Hey, do you want to grab a bite?"

"No, not tonight."

"Oh, hot date, huh?"

"Not really."

Solomon opens his vehicle door. Otis makes his way over to the next lane to his. He looks back and can see the first shifters rushing out of the parking lot. Solomon has his window rolled down, and Otis hollers at him.

"Where is everybody rushing off to?"

"I have no idea, but I have plans of my own. It's me, myself, and I relaxing at home. See you later and stay out of trouble."

Solomon drives off. Otis stands leaning against his vehicle. He pulls out his cell phone and dials a number while mumbling to himself.

"I refuse to be alone tonight. I wonder what everyone else is doing."

Otis pulls out his cell phone and begins to place a call.

*****

Solomon has decided to enjoy his own company tonight. In his home, in comfortable pajamas, with jazz playing softly, Solomon dances around from room to room. Scattered papers, including Aimee's photograph and report, cover the dining room table. As Solomon dances his way from the kitchen to the dining room, he stops to neatly stack the documents. He then places two stacks on nearby shelving.

Gliding to the music, he finds himself in the kitchen again, hovering over a smoking hot skillet. He tosses chopped vegetables in and watches them caramelize. Dropping a thick steak in the middle, his mouth begins to water. The repetitive cycle of dance, season, and taste continues until the edges of the steak itself are crisp. Once he fixes a plate, he finds a comfortable spot on the sofa.

Placing the plate in front of him and grabbing the remote, he turns on the television while turning off the stereo. There are sounds of thunder and flickers of lightning coming through the balcony sliding doors. As Solomon makes his first cut into the steak, suddenly the lights and television go off.

Disappointed, he rises, heads for the kitchen, and rumbles through kitchen drawers to find a candle and matches. He returns to his steak, lights the candle, and sets it on the coffee table. He sits on the floor with legs tucked under the coffee table. Solomon enjoys his dinner by candlelight, alone, and gazing through the glass sliding doors.

*****

On the other side of town, Granny and Agnes hold hands at the kitchen table. While Agnes watches the clock on the wall, Granny says a blessing over the meal.

"Lord, we thank you for this meal and time of sharing. Please continue to draw this family closer together."

"Amen, thank you, Jesus. This looks real good, Momma."

"Don't eat so fast. You don't want to choke. Besides, this is our mother-daughter time together."

"Actually, I'm going out tonight. I promise to spend quality time with you next weekend. Okay, Momma?"

Granny nods her head yes. She does not speak another word.

*****

On the next block, Tyrone is at home alone. He is on his porch and leaning on the banister. Behind him are two chairs and a small table with a stack of photos atop it. A combination of cricket sounds and various genres of music echo from homes and fields in the neighborhood. Slowly, Tyrone turns to take a seat in one of the chairs. He thumbs through the photos, picking one up. It is a photograph of his daughter, Aimee. He rests his face in his hands and cries bitterly.

*****

In the meantime, Pam has a gathering of women in her living room. They are talking loudly, stuffing their faces with junk food, and telling jokes. The phone rings, and she runs to answer it. In the background over the phone, Pam can hear gospel music playing.

"Hello."

"Hey, girl. It's me."

"Crystal? Girl, what's the holdup? You are missing all the fun. Are you coming or what?"

"No, I'm not going to make it tonight. I have studying to do. Next time, okay?"

"Well, okay. I'll see you later then."

Crystal hangs up the phone, turns off the music, and takes a seat on the sofa. On the coffee table in front of her lies a notepad, a pen, and an open Bible.

"Okay, Lord, where were we?"

Pam hangs up the phone, turns to grab two DVDs from a shelf. Holding them up, she turns toward the women.

"Okay, ladies, what's it going to be? *My Best Friend's Wedding* or *Waiting to Exhale?*"

*****

In a restaurant downtown, Victoria and her mom are seated in a booth near a window. Hard rain pounds against the window. They are both holding menus. Victoria places hers aside.

"Mom, do you know what you want?"

Mom is looking around at the full restaurant. It is family night. "No, I haven't looked at my menu yet."

"Mom, you know this menu by heart."

Victoria turns to see what has her mother's attention.

"What are you looking at?"

"Them."

Pastor Sullivan, his wife, adult children, and grandchildren occupy a large section of the dining area. The children are being unruly. Pastor Sullivan and his wife wave. Mom waves back.

"Can you imagine yourself with a bunch of kids and me a grandmother?"

"I don't know about that, Mom. Besides, I need a husband first."

They both burst into laughter.

*****

The rain is subsiding a bit, and just a few miles away, Otis is still in the precinct parking lot. He is trying desperately to make a date. Leaning against his vehicle, he places another call.

"Hey, girl, what's up for tonight? Okay. I'll catch up with you later."

He dials again.

"Sharon? This is Otis. Have you had dinner yet? Oh, okay. Maybe some other time."

Yet another number, this time Otis hears a recording.

"Hello, this is Teresa. Sorry I missed your call. I'm out having a great time. Why aren't you?"

"Good question." Otis puts his phone away, climbs into his vehicle, and slowly cruises down the street. He comes to a stop at a red light. From his window, he catches a glimpse of Victoria and her mother through the restaurant window. They do not see him. He shakes his head and continues driving home.

*****

Later that evening, Solomon is rinsing his dishes at the kitchen sink. The power has not returned; however, there is dim lighting. He picks up the kitchen wall phone and dials Granny's number. On the other side of town, Granny has gone to bed, and Agnes is dressed to party.

She kicks off her shoes and tosses her bag across the room onto the sofa. She plops down into a recliner, with a look of disappointment on her face. The phone rings. Agnes drags herself to a standing position. As she walks toward the phone, she is also removing her jewelry. She answers the phone.

"Phelps residence. Agnes speaking."

"Momma? I can't believe that you are actually at home."

"I do live here, remember?"

"Yes, but you are rarely at home."

"Granny prepared a fantastic dinner for us tonight. I was hoping to get out afterward, but there is no power downtown. We have lights here at the house. Do you?"

"No, just the telephone. Momma, I really need to talk to you. What are you doing tomorrow?"

"Tomorrow night? I have plans."

Suddenly, the lights come on in Solomon's apartment. He stretches the phone's cord to reach Aimee's picture and file. He studies the photograph.

"Well, what about early tomorrow morning? This is important. I've been trying to talk to you for weeks now."

"Okay, okay. If it is that important to you, I'll be here. But don't you have to work tomorrow?"

"This is work, Momma."

Agnes is a little perplexed by his response. Very somberly, she replies, "Yeah, okay. I'll see you early tomorrow morning then, son."

They both hang up. Agnes stands completely still as if in deep thought.

*****

Early the next day, Solomon looks distraught as he enters the front door of Granny's house. Granny is seated in the recliner. Solomon walks right past Granny and neither of them speaks. Granny's eyes follow Solomon to the back of the house. Solomon stops at the entryway of the kitchen. Agnes is seated, having toast and coffee.

"Good morning, son."

"Momma, what can you tell me about Amelia Williams?"

Agnes seems nervous. With her hands shaking, she spills her coffee. She wipes up the spill with a napkin while responding to Solomon's question.

"That was Tyrone Williams' daughter, wasn't she?"

"Was?"

"She ran away or something, didn't she? A long time ago."

Agnes does not look at Solomon. Solomon moves in closer, lifting Agnes's head with his hands. He looks her in the eyes.

"Listen, Momma, I need you to be truthful with me. I talked to Otis, and he said that you and Ruby—"

Agnes interrupts Solomon with a question of her own. "Are you accusing me of something? Are you here to make an arrest?"

"I'm hoping I won't need to. Very few people even know that I am looking at this case. Now, what can you tell me?"

"All right then, son. I'll tell you what I remember."

Agnes emerges and slowly strolls past Solomon. He turns and follows Agnes to the front room. Agnes moves farther ahead, stopping a few feet from the front door. It is old, and the paint is peeling off. Agnes stares at the door as she tells a story that takes Solomon back twenty-five years.

CHAPTER 10

The year is 1972. A younger Agnes, wrapped snugly in outer garments, carries a tray with two cups of hot cocoa on it. She approaches the freshly painted door of Granny's house. A small table is against the wall near the door. Agnes exits onto the front porch. All the homes in the neighborhood are adorned with beautiful Christmas decorations. The grounds, trees, and rooftops are all covered with snow.

Ruby has taken a seat in one of two chairs on the porch. She rises to take a cup from Agnes's tray. She then reclines in her chair, sipping the cocoa. Agnes places the tray on the small table between them then sits back in the other chair as the two of them critique the individual homes, trying to decide which is the most beautiful, creative, and unique.

They also share local gossip. As they are finishing their cocoa, they realize how much time has passed. Ruby rises and rushes down the front steps and across the street toward her house. Agnes hollers out to her.

"Wait, where are you going?"

"I have to check on my cornbread. I could burn my house down fooling around with you. I have collards slow cooking too. I'll bring you some."

Ruby rushes into her home, closing the door behind her. Agnes leans forward to see that Aimee is drawing closer. She has already gathered her purse's contents and is nearing the front of Granny's house. Agnes calls out to her.

"Hey, Little Miss. Aimee."

Aimee squints her eyes and sees the city bus at a distance. It pulls to the curb to load and off-load passengers. It then pulls off and out of sight.

"Dang it. I missed my bus. Oh, hey, Ms. Phelps. How are you?"

Agnes moves down the stairs and to the front gate. "Your daddy acts like he doesn't even know me anymore. Tell him I said hello."

"Tell him yourself."

Aimee picks up her pace. "Wait a second. I have something for you."

"Ms. Phelps, I told you—"

Agnes opens the gate, holding it for Aimee. And interrupting, she says, "This is not about me. It's a Christmas gift from Solomon. It will only take a second."

Aimee follows Agnes into the house. As they step inside, Agnes walks to the rear of the home while Aimee stands waiting in the dimly lit front room. Agnes fades into the darkness. Aimee observes the home decor. She steps in closer to see family pictures on the walls. She calls out to Agnes.

"Does Solomon even know that he has a sister?"

Agnes does not answer. Startled by a rambling sound, Aimee turns to see shadows from the kitchen. Agnes is opening and closing cabinets and drawers.

"Ms. Phelps, I only have a minute. Come on."

Agnes reemerges from the rear of the home. Aimee is stunned by Agnes's presence and a poking in her back. Aimee shudders. She realizes that it is a gun. Agnes speaks softly.

"Nothing personal."

Agnes pulls the trigger, instantly killing Aimee. Her body hits the floor. Agnes is stunned and stands there with the gun in her hand. She just stares at the gun in disbelief. She tucks the gun behind her back and tiptoes to Solomon's room, peaking in. He is sound asleep.

Agnes was happy that Granny was away for the weekend at a church retreat. Agnes returns to the front room and drags Aimee's body to the back door. She can hear the front door opening. It is Ruby, carrying a plate. She enters calling out to Agnes.

"Agnes, I brought you some collards and cornbread."

Ruby sets the plate down on the table near the front door. Agnes abruptly appears from the back room of the house, startling Ruby.

"Keep your voice down, Ruby."

"Why is it so dark in here, and why are we whispering?"

Agnes grabs Ruby by both wrists pulling her in and staring into her eyes.

"I've always had your back on everything, right?"

Ruby looks puzzled and reluctantly responds, "Yeah?"

"Well, I need to know that you have mine this time."

"Agnes, what are you talking about?"

Holding on to one of Ruby's hands, Agnes leads her to the kitchen and then turns on the light. Agnes covers her own mouth with both hands and backs away, resting against the wall. A blood-streaked plastic mat spans the length of the floor, from the front room to the back door. At the end of the mat lies the lifeless body of Aimee. Agnes is sniffling. Ruby is frantic.

"Agnes, what have you done?"

"You have to help me, Ruby."

"And what is it that you expect me to do? We have to call the police."

Ruby rushes to grab the house phone. Agnes and Ruby tussle for the phone. Ruby drops the phone, and they both dive to get it. Once on the floor, Ruby checks Aimee's pulse. Agnes grabs the phone, hanging it up.

"We are not calling the police."

"We? I don't have anything to do with this. I hope this was an accident. You didn't mean to kill her, did you, Agnes?"

Agnes shakes her head no.

"Let me call the police, Agnes. You can explain to them what happened."

"You seriously want to have me arrested, don't you? Don't forget I know some things about you, like all that money you embezzled from the company we both worked for."

"Please, you can't even begin to compare that to what has happened here?"

"It's still prison time regardless. And I have a lot more on you than that, and you know it."

There is a staring match between Ruby and Agnes. When that passes, they both begin a rigorous cleanup job. They begin by rolling and wrapping Aimee tightly in the plastic mat. Together, they carry Aimee's bundled body from the rear of the home, through the alley, and to the back of the abandoned house on the end of the block. They drop her several times.

It is a very dark and quiet night. Just on the outside of the gate that surrounds the boarded-up old house is a large garbage dumpster. On the inside of the yard, a new tool shed stands firm. They pass these and decide to put the body inside the old house. Once inside, they put her down and look for a place to hide the body. Ruby trips over some loose floorboards.

They remove several, then drag the body, and dump it underneath. Agnes takes the gun from her jacket's inner pocket. She tucks it inside the plastic wrap with Aimee's body. They replace the floorboards and rush out and back to Granny's house. Upon arrival at Granny's house, Agnes looks in on Solomon again. He is still sound asleep. The two spend hours cleaning and scrubbing the bloodstains.

*****

Present day

Solomon stares at Agnes. He is distraught over what he has learned. Granny is collapsed in the recliner and appears to be asleep. Agnes walks past Solomon and back into the kitchen. She pours herself another cup of coffee as if all is well. Solomon uses his cell phone to make a call. He speaks softly.

"It's worse than I thought. How soon can you get here?"

Solomon ends the call and returns to the kitchen where Agnes is now seated. She takes a sip of coffee and then continues.

"I wish Ruby hadn't left that night. I did not want to kill that girl. Believe it or not, I was thinking of you."

"Me? That doesn't make sense."

"You deserved more than Tyrone was giving, and she was in the way. Basically, that's it."

"You didn't have to kill her. I always thought her face was familiar, but I never really knew who she was. You killed my sister."

"Your daddy should have given you more."

"No, Momma. He is a very generous man. You're upset because he didn't choose you."

"I can't believe you just said that. I did bear his child, you know. He could have helped me out a little more. That's all I'm trying to say."

"See, Momma, I knew this wasn't about me."

"How old were you, son, when Granny finally told you that Tyrone was your father."

"First of all, you should have been the one to tell me that. Granny didn't have to tell me. Pops had his own way of letting me know that."

*****

Back in the day, eight-year-old Otis and Solomon are working diligently to clean the shop. Solomon notices that Tyrone's office door is cracked open slightly. He moves toward the office peeking in. There are several colorful helium balloons floating side to side on strings near Tyrone's desk.

Solomon pushes the door open and approaches the desk; Otis follows him. Solomon climbs into Tyrone's chair. Solomon grins ear to ear as he reads the writing on top of a cake. "Happy eighth Birthday, Solomon." Numerous wrapped gifts cover the desktop. Tyrone appears at the door.

"You boys can finish by cleaning this office. I'm going to drop these gifts and things off at Granny's house, and then I will be back. Don't forget to act surprised when you see it all later."

"Thanks, Pops."

"You're welcome, and happy birthday, Solomon."

Later that afternoon, at Granny's house, Solomon rushes in to see the same birthday cake and gifts now on Granny's dining room table. He is startled by his mother's voice.

"Solomon, did you have to go and spoil my surprise? Get dressed, all of the kids will be here soon."

Solomon dips his finger in the frosting, tasting it, before going to his bedroom. Agnes continues to speak.

"You know I would never forget my baby's birthday. You are going to love all of the presents I bought for you."

Solomon stops in his tracks, looking back.

"Oh, yes, right. Thanks."

"One day you are going to have everything, baby. Just don't forget about your Momma when you get it."

Solomon appalled, shakes his head as he enters his room.

*****

Present day

Agnes and Solomon continue their conversation at the kitchen table. Agnes responds to Solomon's story about the birthday surprise.

"Well, it was the least he could have done for you."

"You always tried to take credit for the things he did for me. Back to the subject at hand, please help me understand what you stood to gain by killing Aimee. It makes no sense."

"At the time, it seemed to. Tyrone was always a very sickly man. I am surprised that cancer didn't take him out the first time. I was thinking he would soon die, and with Aimee out of the way, we would get everything. But he beat that cancer."

"I'm ashamed of you. Granny was always more of a mother to me than you were anyway."

"That's not true. Solomon, you know I love you."

"You never had time for me. And what you did to my sister. There is no justification for that, so stop making excuses."

Agnes rolls her eyes at Solomon. She stands and moves to the back window. Pulling back the curtain, she stares down the path to the yard where the abandoned house once stood. She reminisces.

"That was twenty-five years ago. Why are you bringing it up now?"

"It's my job. It was God's will that I was the one who found her. Was it guilt that made you mark the grave?"

"What? There's a grave marker for her? That must have been Ruby on one of her drinking binges. At least I hope it was. I don't think anyone saw us."

Agnes returns to her seat, oblivious to the severity of her situation. Solomon's cell phone rings, and he moves to the front room to answer it.

"Yes, I'm as ready as I'll ever be. Just come alone, okay?"

For the next forty-five minutes, Solomon paces the floor from the kitchen in the rear, to the front door, and back again. It felt like hours. Each time he reaches the front door, he would look out and down the street for Otis. Finally, Otis pulls up in front, driving the black luxury vehicle that he and Solomon cruised the neighborhood in for the past decade or so. Otis slowly approaches Granny's home, climbing the stairs.

Solomon greets him with an embrace. Neither of them speaks as they walk through the house and into the kitchen where Otis pulls out handcuffs. He puts them on Agnes. A very teary-eyed emotional Solomon takes Agnes by one arm, with Otis taking her other. They make the arrest, escorting Agnes to the vehicle outside.

Granny is now awake, and she watches them pass her in the living room and out the front door. Granny does not say a word but follows them outside. Solomon helps his mother into the back seat of the vehicle. Granny watches from the porch. As the vehicle pulls off, Granny drops her head and enters her home.

CHAPTER
11

The next day, in downtown Detroit, Bernard Burgess gazes from his high-rise apartment window. He has a complete view of rooftops, the downtown area, and residential streets. He is sipping on a can of SlimFast. The interior of his apartment is very neat and modest. A television is in the center of the space and blares the local news. The story draws Bernard in closer. The reporter on the screen is standing in front of the vacant lot in the old neighborhood. He listens intently as she speaks.

"Police and detectives are on site today, hoping to exhume the remains of Amelia Williams. She was reported missing over twenty-five years ago."

Bernard moves from the television to the fireplace. On the mantel are several framed photographs. One old photo is of three eight-year-old boys standing outside of Granny's house. It is a photograph of Solomon, Otis, and Bernard. He stares at the picture and reminisces about those days. Once again, the reporter's words get Bernard's attention. With the framed picture in his hand, he moves in toward the television to hear the rest of the story. He sees the reporter standing with Solomon, and the reporter continues.

"We spoke with Detective Solomon Phelps, in charge of the investigation, and this is what he had to say."

"I grew up on this very street. Solving this case will finally bring closure for many people and families in this community."

Bernard removes the picture from the frame and turns it over. Written on the back of it is "The Three Musketeers"—Bernard, Otis, and Solomon. Bernard tucks the picture in his shirt pocket, grabs a jacket, and heads out toward the elevator. He rushes to the parking lot and jumps in his convertible, letting the top down. He takes one final glance at the picture and places it in his pocket. He blasts old-school music as he pulls off in a hurry.

Bernard arrives on the site of the exhumation, parking on the opposite side of the street. The noise from the heavy equipment has drawn people from neighboring streets as well. Bernard crosses the street and blends in with the onlookers. He spots both Otis and Solomon conversing on the grounds. Gus wants to be a part of the action, so he is tagging along with Otis and Solomon. Gus walks away from Otis and Solomon and, with a notepad and paper, approaches two women standing with the onlookers. Otis points him out to Solomon.

"Look at Leggs over there, trying to play detective."

"That's fine. It'll give him something to do."

"Seriously, Solomon? He is doing more flirting than investigating."

Solomon is more focused on the investigation. Otis is trying to defuse the situation, by making fun of Gus. He hollers out to Gus.

"Hey, Officer Leggs! Officer Harry Leggs!"

Gus, obviously annoyed, waves and then turns his attention back to the women. Otis has failed at his attempt to calm Solomon.

"Leggs heard me that time. Come on, Solomon. I'm just trying to cheer you up."

"Yes, O. I know. Try to take this a little more seriously."

"Believe it or not, Solomon. I know how serious this is. But this could turn out bad. We may have both of our family names dragged through the dirt."

"Only the ones that are dirty. Do you think I'm not feeling the brunt of this? Think again, but I have a job to do."

"Ms. Agnes is your mother. Was there no other way?"

"Aimee was my sister; and what about answers for my pops? What would you have done?"

"I'm not sure. I'm glad I didn't have that decision to make."

Otis drops his head and walks away. Several onlookers whisper and point fingers. They dig the grounds for hours, daylight begins to fade, and the onlookers start to dissipate. Solomon approaches Otis.

"We've overturned the entire site. So where is she?"

Otis shrugs his shoulders and turns to the crew. "That's it. Let's wrap it up."

"No, not yet. Wait a minute, Otis."

Solomon notices Bernard standing on the opposite end of the lot, nearest to the alley. Bernard motions to Solomon, pointing toward the alley. Solomon hollers at the crew.

"Everyone, sit tight for a second."

Solomon walks across the lot, meeting Bernard. The tool shed is sitting at an angle between the lot and the alley. It is old, rusty, and a bit mangled. An overflowing garbage dumpster sits close by. Solomon tears the shed open. Wrapped loosely in a long yellowed plastic mat are the tattered clothing and skeletal remains of Amelia Williams. Solomon mumbles.

"How could she have been here all this time?"

Bernard moves in closer.

Solomon studies him for a moment, then expresses, "I remember you."

"Yes, and I remember you too."

Bernard removes the photograph of Otis, Solomon, and himself from his jacket pocket, showing it to Solomon. They both ponder the events of the night Aimee's body was discovered in the boarded-up old abandoned house.

*****

On that cold winter night in 1972, eight-year-old Solomon and Otis stand over the corpse of Amelia Williams (aka Aimee). They take off running, exiting through the front door, and down the street to Granny's house. Shortly thereafter, eight-year-old Bernard enters the abandoned house from the rear.

"Otis! Solomon! Are you guys in here?"

Young Bernard searches through the house, looking for Otis and Solomon. He finds the corpse of Aimee. Frightened, Bernard runs out the back door. He climbs the fence to his house next door. Bernard's home is the small house that sits between Granny's house and the boarded-up old house on the corner.

He runs into his house and to his room, closing the door. His mother hears him come in. She opens his door. She is combing her hair as she gets ready for work. She reaches in one of his dresser drawers, then tosses a clean set of pajamas on his bed.

"I had no idea you were still outside playing. Get dressed for bed, Bernard. Your dinner is on the table, so hurry up before it gets cold."

"Yes, ma'am."

Mrs. Burgess exits to dress herself for work. Hoping he is not in trouble for staying out too late, he fails to mention that he has been in the abandoned house next door. Bernard enters the dining room and climbs into a chair. He scuffs down beef stew and cornbread, washing it down with a tall glass of grape Kool-Aid. As his mother bundles in her outer garments, Bernard climbs out of the chair and walks her to the front door. She grabs the doorknob and turns toward Bernard.

"You know the rules. Do not answer the phone, don't look out the window, and don't answer the door. Understand?"

"Yes, ma'am."

"Now where is my hug?"

"Good night, Momma."

Bernard leaps into his mother's arms for a warm hug. His mother, with keys in her hands, points Bernard in the direction of the den. A sofa sleeper, fluffed with pillows, blankets, and toys, sits just in front of a small television. He runs, diving onto the sleeper. Laughing, he waves goodbye to his mother. Still looking back, she says, "You can watch television in the den tonight but keep it down. Ms. Taylor is going to be a little late. She can let herself in."

"Okay, Momma."

"It won't be much longer, baby. When I get that day job across town, we can move away from here and have more time together. Okay, baby?"

Bernard nods yes with an ear-to-ear smile. They both blow kisses, and his mother exits, locking the door behind her. Later that evening, with Ms. Taylor asleep on a chair, Bernard hears a noise from the backside of the house. He peels the curtain back slightly.

Ruby and Agnes carry a large bundle from the back exit of the abandoned house to its backyard and then into the shed. Little Bernard is careful not to let them see him. He watches them struggle to carry the load. He can vaguely hear them talking. Ruby whispers to Agnes, "When this snow clears up. She's going to stink."

"With all this garbage back here, who would even notice."

"Agnes, you are a psychopath. Poor Ms. Aimee. Why are we moving her anyway?"

"They're going to tear that house down soon. If we are lucky, no one will look in here. This neighborhood has been neglected for years, and this tool shed is like new."

"That doesn't mean they won't look in here."

"It's the chance I have to take until I can figure something else out."

They stumble, dropping Aimee's body. Ruby grabs the corpse, hugging her.

"I'm so sorry, Ms. Aimee. I'm so sorry."

Bernard can clearly hear the name Ms. Aimee. He whispers it to himself.

"Ms. Aimee."

Agnes pulls Ruby away from the embrace. "Come on now, Ruby. We have to finish this."

Agnes and Ruby shove the bundle into the shed and shut it securely. Agnes pulls a lock from inside her jacket, further securing the shed. They try to be quiet as they make their way back through the alley and into Granny's house. Bernard gently closes the curtain and then tiptoes to his room. He takes a seat at a small desk that has various art supplies on top of it. On the desk are a miniature set of carving tools, a stack of small wood canvases, tiny stakes, paints, coloring books, crayons, scissors, glue, and a pair of craft man gloves.

A sardine can on the desktop contains the carcass of a small bird. One of the small wooden canvases has "Mr. Bird" carved in and painted on it. Securely attached to the back of the small canvas are two stakes: one on each side. Bernard begins to carve Aimee on another small canvas. He peeks through his bedroom door to see that Ms. Taylor is still asleep and snoring loudly. He returns to his craft table to complete a tombstone for Aimee. When he finishes the tiny grave markers, he climbs into his bed and falls asleep.

Early the next morning, Bernard arises and investigates the living room. Ms. Taylor is gone. Bernard peeks into his mother's room, finding her asleep. He rushes to his room, bundles in outer garments, and heads outside. He is carrying the sardine can with the dead bird inside, two tiny grave markers, and a toy shovel.

Bernard carries these items into the backyard of the boarded-up house. He digs a deep hole, to bury Mr. Bird, firmly pressing the stakes into the ground. He then walks over to the shed and tries to secure a marker for Aimee, but it keeps falling over. He returns to the site for Mr. Bird and firmly secures a marker for Aimee nearby. He stands there admiring his work, then climbs over the fence back into his own backyard.

Two weeks later, Bernard and his mother pack up to move to the other side of town. Solomon and Otis are standing on Granny's porch waving goodbye. Bernard's mother drives past with Bernard waving from the rear window. They are following behind a moving van. They continue driving until out of sight.

*****

Present day

On the vacant lot, Bernard and Solomon exchange smiles and handshakes. They continue their conversation. Solomon recalls it all and responds, "Little Bernie. Do you still live around here?"

"Downtown."

"Why didn't you tell somebody about this before now?"

"I had no idea this case went unsolved until today. You know I have been hoping to make the academy. Do you think I have a shot?"

"Helping me find Ms. Williams was a good start. I have to wrap this up right now, but I'm sure we can talk about it later."

CHAPTER 12

The next few months would prove trying for Solomon. He would have to reexamine his life and seek God on his purpose. And in doing so, he will discover that at times, the seasons in our lives do overlap. It is common to have more than one calling in life. Sometimes, seasons change; and other times, they coincide.

By the time Solomon had addressed all his issues and confronted all his fears, he realized the necessity for his multifunctional position in his family and the community. He had arrested Agnes while finding her a good attorney, given closure to Tyrone, helped with memorial services for Amelia, and found more time to spend with Granny and taking her on visits to the prison to pray for Agnes. He had even begun to form a better relationship with his mother, albeit, from behind prison walls.

*****

Three Years Later

A large crowd pours into the front doors of House of Praise Christian Ministries. Inside, the sanctuary is full.

The congregation and choir jubilantly sing praises. On the wall near the main entrance hangs a large framed portrait of now-deceased Pastor Sullivan. The inscription below reads, "Beloved Pastor of Forty Years, Oscar Sullivan."

Among the congregation are Tyrone, Otis, Pam, and Granny. Victoria leads a song from the choir stand. As the song is ending, the pastor's voice can be heard. The speaker is Pastor Solomon Phelps.

"If this is your first time worshipping with us, myself, my lovely wife—"

As Solomon mentions his wife, a conservatively dressed Crystal rises to her feet. She is on the front pew, trying to juggle an infant and a toddler. She manages to wave at the congregation.

"—and our church family welcome you. Please stand for the reading of God's holy word."

The congregation all stand, with Bibles in their hands. Pastor Solomon Phelps reads from the book of Ecclesiastes.

"Ecclesiastes, chapter 3. There is a time for everything and a SEASON for every activity under heaven."

The end!

About the Author

Terry McBride was born and raised in Detroit, Michigan. Writing had always been a hobby of hers. In her youth, she created funny stories that she shared with her friends. In her teens, she kept a journal of her thoughts, usually in the form of poetry. She accepted Jesus at the age of fifteen. After graduating high school, Terry joined the air force and was a part of the air force's traveling entertainment showcase, *Tops in Blue*. Here, she found a new way to share funny stories through a comical four-year-old character, which she created, named Tomika. Terry later studied business and media productions at American InterContinental University. She is a screenwriter and a novelist, and it is her hope that her writing will be inspiring as well as entertaining.

CPSIA information can be obtained
at www.ICGtesting.com
Printed in the USA
JSHW031623210622
27250JS00001B/8